W9-AVS-894

Wyatt had everything going for him, looks-wise

If he'd been off work because of illness, Casey couldn't tell. He was robust, tan and all-around fit. She'd admired the ripple of muscles when he bent to change filters. From any angle he was attractive.

Not that how he looked mattered. What mattered was if he liked the photos she'd taken today.

But still, she wondered why he'd closed a studio that was producing at its peak. She'd never pry, but she was curious. What did he have to hide?

Guessing served no purpose. She just needed to dig in and do a good job. She and Wyatt could swap life stories later if they lasted as a team. Her energy would be better spent thinking about what he might say once she could no longer conceal her pregnancy.

Dear Reader,

This is a special year for Harlequin readers and the authors of Harlequin books. It is the 60th anniversary of a company we all love. Which is fitting, because Harlequin publishes wonderful stories about love that are read worldwide.

I grew up in a small rural town that was lucky enough to have an extensive library. For avid readers like me, my sister and our friends, books—Harlequin books in particular—opened up our otherwise narrow view of the world. Harlequin stories have always been about two people falling in love—a love that lasts for all eternity. But they're more. The books show glimpses of real life, from small towns to exotic locales. And they're stories about possibilities. Harlequin characters give readers hope that hardships can be overcome, and that women, especially, can be anything they want to be.

I felt more than fortunate in 1989 when editor Paula Eykelhof bought my first book for the Harlequin Romance line. Since then I've been privileged to write for Harlequin Superromance, Harlequin American Romance and other special productions. All the editors and staff at Harlequin are dedicated to publishing quality books, and I'm so very proud to be part of the greater Harlequin family.

As always, I enjoyed writing Casey Sinclair and Wyatt Keene's love story. It's also nice to get letters from readers. I hope you all remain satisfied readers through many more milestones in Harlequin's history.

Thank you,

Roz Denny Fox
rdfox@cox.net
7739 E. Broadway Blvd. #101
Tucson, AZ 85710-3941

The Baby Album
Roz Denny Fox

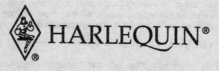

TORONTO • NEW YORK • LONDON
AMSTERDAM • PARIS • SYDNEY • HAMBURG
STOCKHOLM • ATHENS • TOKYO • MILAN • MADRID
PRAGUE • WARSAW • BUDAPEST • AUCKLAND

If you purchased this book without a cover you should be aware that this book is stolen property. It was reported as "unsold and destroyed" to the publisher, and neither the author nor the publisher has received any payment for this "stripped book."

Recycling programs
for this product may
not exist in your area.

ISBN-13: 978-0-373-71586-2

THE BABY ALBUM

Copyright © 2009 by Rosaline D. Fox.

All rights reserved. Except for use in any review, the reproduction or utilization of this work in whole or in part in any form by any electronic, mechanical or other means, now known or hereafter invented, including xerography, photocopying and recording, or in any information storage or retrieval system, is forbidden without the written permission of the publisher, Harlequin Enterprises Limited, 225 Duncan Mill Road, Don Mills, Ontario, Canada M3B 3K9.

This is a work of fiction. Names, characters, places and incidents are either the product of the author's imagination or are used fictitiously, and any resemblance to actual persons, living or dead, business establishments, events or locales is entirely coincidental.

This edition published by arrangement with Harlequin Books S.A.

® and TM are trademarks of the publisher. Trademarks indicated with ® are registered in the United States Patent and Trademark Office, the Canadian Trade Marks Office and in other countries.

www.eHarlequin.com

Printed in U.S.A.

ABOUT THE AUTHOR

Roz Denny Fox has been a RITA® Award finalist
and has placed in a number of other contests; her
books have also appeared on the Waldenbooks
bestseller list. She's happy to have received her
twenty-five-book pin with Harlequin Books and
would one day love to get the pin for fifty books.
Roz currently resides in Tucson, Arizona, with her
husband, Denny. They have two daughters.

Books by Roz Denny Fox

For Nakita and Savannah, ace divers,
great softball players and, best of all,
avid readers. Dream big, girls.
Reach for the stars.

CHAPTER ONE

CASEY SINCLAIR PULLED into the high school parking lot. Should she park and go in? She was half an hour early for her job interview, but hadn't wanted to be late if there was traffic on the road from Round Rock, Texas, to Austin. She'd been hesitant—a school was an odd place to interview a photographer, after all—but the e-mail she'd received June 1st had explained that it was a working interview. Casey would take part in a photo shoot and would be paid for her time.

Eager as she was to do a good job, Casey felt like crap today. Morning sickness. Day two of it. Maybe it was payback for having deliberately left out any mention of her pregnancy in the cover letter she'd sent with her résumé. But she'd been afraid of having her application rejected on that basis. Besides, at the time she'd felt perfectly fine. Now, not so much.

Just this week, a nurse practitioner at the free clinic in Round Rock had listed several possible symptoms Casey might experience during her pregnancy, including morning sickness. Yesterday, when she'd woken up, nauseous, she'd told herself it was the power of suggestion. When she was sick again this morning, she was forced to admit it might be for real. So all she'd eaten for breakfast were half a dozen soda crackers. And she hadn't made any sudden moves, as the nurse advised.

Now, hours later, she still felt nauseated.

It could be butterflies because of this interview, but she had to get over it. She needed this job badly. Right before she left home this morning, someone from the electric company had called and said if she didn't pay her bill ASAP, they'd turn off her power. She'd said she was expecting some money after today, and the rep had agreed to give her an extension until Monday.

Taking a deep breath, Casey climbed out of the twelve-year-old Honda her soon-to-be-ex-husband had left behind when he took off. No doubt Dane hadn't thought he could sell it.

Casey eyed the almost bald tire nearest her and wondered how much longer she could put off replacing them all. Thank heavens the e-mail had said she'd receive at least fifty dollars for helping the studio owner with his team photographs. The money was more than welcome, but wouldn't stretch far. Casey needed a regular income.

She retrieved her trusted Nikon, her light meter and her purse from the backseat, then shut the door with her hip.

She prayed for a good outcome as she walked toward the gymnasium, crossing her fingers that her stomach would settle and that she'd do everything the interviewer asked of her perfectly. She noticed parents pulling up to drop their kids at the door.

The cavernous, brightly lit space looked like all high school gymnasiums. Noise ricocheted off the high ceilings. Across the room, two men stood near the bleachers, talking and gesturing. Boys and girls in a variety of uniforms were horsing around. A few straggled in from what Casey guessed were the locker rooms.

Her attention skidded back to the men. One wore gray sweats, the other khaki slacks and a short-sleeve pullover. The second man claimed the bulk of Casey's interest, because even as he spoke, he was busy assembling two light stands and a tripod.

Wyatt Keene. That was who Casey was supposed to meet today. The ad she'd found had given no information at all about the prospective employer. A few lines in the Help Wanted section of the Austin paper simply stated "Photographer wanted for studio portraits and off-site work. Prefer experience with weddings and family groups."

Casey had experience.

She'd also had a week to get used to Wyatt Keene's name, and to do a little research. There was a Keene Photography Studio listed in the phone book, which went a long way toward easing her mind about meeting a strange man in a school gym.

Tightening her grip on her camera, she headed toward the pair, hoping against hope that Wyatt Keene would be as nice as his name felt rolling off her tongue.

"Mr. Keene." At the sound of Casey's voice, the man holding the equipment wheeled abruptly toward her. She smiled and extended her hand. "I'm Casey Sinclair. I'm sorry I'm early, but there was much less traffic than I expected. Anyway, I always say it's better to be early than late."

Casey felt her smile fade under the man's frowning scrutiny. *Heavens!* Was it a crime to show up early? Or did he think she was too chatty? She tended to babble when she was nervous. And boy, was she nervous. The man kept staring at her with eyes that were even blacker than his hair, and not very friendly. "Are you Wyatt Keene?" she asked hesitantly, tempering her earlier enthusiasm.

"Yes. This is Mike Granville, the coach. We'll be taking team photos today for the yearbook. The captains have props they want to display, and Mike wants us to use trophies. Bats, balls and such. Or signs with the sport's insignia. In the past I've had the captains kneel in front of their teams. I told Mike I'll take the first photo of his soccer squads. The most difficult job will be getting the kids to stop fooling around. Otherwise, it's standard picture-taking protocol."

Casey opened her mouth to say she understood, but Keene went on with his instructions. "Watch me from the bleachers. You'll see what I mean. When I'm done, you can shoot the swim team. Five or six frames ought to be enough. If I think you've done okay, you can photograph the varsity and junior varsity baseball players."

He spun without another word, picked up his gear

and strode across the gym. Casey heard him call out to boys and girls in soccer uniforms.

What a hard nose! Even the coach must have thought so, because he offered Casey a sympathetic glance before heading off to tell a group of noisy boys to be quiet.

The real pity of it, Casey thought, was that Keene was darn good-looking, with his angular jaw, brooding jet-black eyes and a stubbled chin that was at odds with his almost military-short haircut. She guessed he might be thirtyish. He was probably an inch over six feet, which made her feel much shorter than her five-foot-two height warranted. The photographer had the build of a natural athlete. Not too thin, muscular or bulky, but just right in her estimation.

His attitude left a lot to be desired, though. Casey ground her teeth as she hurried after him. If she hadn't been so desperate for this job, she would've walked out right then.

She pulled up short directly behind Keene as he fumbled the tilt head he was screwing to a tripod. Casey grabbed for the delicate piece of equipment and their hands collided.

"What are you doing?" He all but leaped away. "I said take a seat in the bleachers where you can watch the first group shot."

"Yes, sir," she said, annoyed by his attitude. She slapped the tilt head into his hand and stomped off to take a seat.

Part of her fumed. But her heart also pounded at

being chastised for trying to be helpful. Keene acted as if he'd rather not breathe the same air. Her stomach got all jittery again. What was his problem? She'd been counting on this job, but now… Disappointment crept in. It was patently obvious that he'd taken an instant dislike to her. Casey hadn't the faintest idea why. She glanced down at her capris and sandals. Was she dressed too casually? She'd thought it was important to be able to move comfortably for the shoot, but maybe Keene had expected something more professional.

At her foster parents' studio in Dallas, she'd even worn jeans on field shoots. But then, Len and Dolly Howell were good-hearted people. They'd offered to come down here and help her move straight back home with them when she'd called to let them know Dane had left her. If they had any inkling she was pregnant and almost broke, they wouldn't wait for an invitation; they'd be here. Which was why she couldn't tell them. Not only were both getting on in years, but they'd already helped her more than enough. It was time for her to stand on her own two feet.

Casey flopped down on the hard bleachers and studied the gym more thoroughly. When would the other applicants arrive? Surely she wasn't the only person vying for this job. She'd planned to make such a stunning first impression that Keene would automatically want to hire her. Apparently she'd blown that in the first five minutes.

With her purse and camera balanced on her lap, she

settled her chin stubbornly on her hands. She would show Keene she was the best person for this job.

WYATT DIDN'T RELAX UNTIL a sidelong glance revealed that Casey Sinclair had found a spot off the court. He shouldn't have growled at her, but he'd been thrown off stride. First by her breezy warmth, but more by the touch of her hand brushing his.

He'd told Greg Moore, his best friend and business accountant, that he wasn't comfortable with the fact that only two of the thirty applicants had enough experience to fill Angela's shoes. The other qualified applicant had placed too many conditions and restrictions on what he wanted in a job for Wyatt to even consider contacting him for an interview. Wyatt knew it shouldn't be relevant, but he wished his one viable candidate wasn't so attractive. Her eyes—well, suffice it to say they drew a man in. And Wyatt didn't need that kind of complication after the awful year he'd had.

He massaged his chest and motioned for the first soccer team to gather around. He spent a few minutes arranging the kids by height for a better composition. When he stepped behind his camera, a long forgotten burst of pleasure came roaring back. It felt good to be getting on with work he loved.

Greg had been right to prod and badger him. Wyatt had frittered away a year during which he took no paying jobs. Looking back, the busywork he'd done, like painting his house inside and out and refinishing the bedroom set Angela had wanted him to do, hadn't given him any satisfaction. In fact, as soon as it was completed he'd advertised on Craigslist and had given the set away. Throughout that time he'd avoided his friends and drifted—until Greg said that if he didn't snap out of his grief, he'd risk losing his house and the studio he'd poured so much money into. The studio he'd built for Angela.

Really, Wyatt had no choice but to give Casey Sinclair the opportunity to show what she could do. He needed her. According to her résumé, and the references he'd got from her previous employer in Dallas, she had all the skills he needed to get Keene Studio up and running. And that had to be Wyatt's focus now.

COACH GRANVILLE CAME OVER and sat down next to Casey as Wyatt took shot after shot of the soccer teams. "I dread picture days," he lamented. "The kids are antsy to get it over with. I've always liked Wyatt's work. He gets the job done, and has a knack for dealing with kids. I for one am happy he's opening his studio again. Last year I had to work with another firm. That photographer had zero rapport with teenagers, and the pictures reflected it. I can't tell you how many calls I fielded from unhappy parents."

Casey cut her gaze from Wyatt to the coach. "His studio's been closed? I wasn't aware of that. He advertised in the *Austin American-Statesman*. I assumed he'd lost a photographer, or that the business needed extra help."

Granville gnawed his lip, abruptly clamming up. It

was obvious he'd rather not tell her any more about Wyatt Keene. While Casey search for something to say, he bolted from his seat.

"All I can tell you is Wyatt had valid reasons for taking a hiatus," he said. Then the coach was gone, rustling up a gaggle of boys shooting baskets at the far end of the gym.

Keene had finished with the soccer players and Casey realized he was gesturing for her to take over. She couldn't shake Coach Granville's comment. *The studio hadn't been open in a year.* Had Wyatt Keene been ill? If so, that might account for his brusqueness. Maybe he didn't feel well. She could definitely sympathize with that.

She left her seat, more determined than ever to do an exceptional job. Still, she was a bit concerned about working for someone whose studio had been closed for a year. Would he have enough clients to warrant paying her what she needed to support herself? Supposing she even wanted to spend eight or more hours a day around another jerk of a man.

After what she'd just gone through with Dane, it might be smarter to cut her losses and seek another job. Although she already knew jobs in her field weren't easy to come by. It was too costly to consider opening her own studio. And it was too painful to admit her naïveté when it came to Dane. Back home in Dallas, a lot of her girlfriends had got married straight out of college. Not Casey. She'd insisted on holding out for

Mr. Absolutely Right. When she met Dane a couple of years after graduating, she'd thought she'd found him.

Ha! What a joke.

She couldn't—wouldn't—go back to Dallas with her life in shambles, she thought as she waited for the swim team to gather. And the other jobs she'd found in the paper weren't suitable for a woman in her condition. House painting at a new real estate development. Not with the dizziness she'd experienced these past two days. And the fumes wouldn't be good for her baby.

She'd answered an ad for two payroll clerks. It turned out to be for a chemical company on the far outskirts of Austin. Chemical residue and odors would be bad for her child, too. Growing desperate, she'd toyed with the idea of applying to be a pet sitter for two dogs, since she liked animals. But the job didn't pay enough to cover the cost of the gas for the thirty mile round trip to Austin every day.

This job, working for the unfriendly Wyatt Keene, matched her schooling, her experience and her interests to a T. Casey had worked in her foster parents' studio since high school. She'd loved every second of it. Still did, she admitted to herself as she clicked several practice shots. Len Howell had taught her how to take beautiful family and wedding portraits—which was how she'd met Dane. Howell Studios had been hired to photograph Dane's sister's wedding, and he'd been the best man. From the outset, Dane had been oh, so charming. That first day he'd jokingly called her Pixie, since even in heels she barely reached his chin. And back then her blond hair had been styled in short, feathery wisps.

Now it badly needed cutting, but there hadn't been enough money, she acknowledged, tugging on one of the shoulder-length strands before she started corralling the group of giggling swimmers.

As for *her* first assessment of Dane Sinclair, she'd been infatuated.

Glaring at Wyatt Keene's broad back, Casey was determined not to be infatuated again. Because a handsome face and hard body didn't make a good man. Dane had proven that. Uncharacteristically swept off her feet, Casey had leaped to accept his request for a date. They'd gone out exclusively for several months. By then she'd fallen in love. Love had changed her. Made her less serious and more impulsive. So when Dane announced one day that he'd bought a brewpub in Round Rock, Texas, from an old frat buddy, was it any wonder her heart had sunk at the mere suggestion of his leaving Dallas? Leaving her?

Even now she could hear him say, "Pixie, it'll be a blast selling brewskis. You know how my folks are always insisting I get a job. Well, my dad's going to buy me a microbrewery. It's the perfect solution."

"What about us, Dane?" she'd asked. It was still painful to recall how badly she'd wanted him to ask her to marry him then and there. Instead, he'd avoided meeting her gaze and made excuses to leave.

It wasn't until the next day that he casually suggested she drive to Round Rock in a week or two. "To help check out my inventory. And hang out for a while," he'd added, throwing in one of his trademark magnetic smiles.

Dane never brought up marriage. So she had. She'd been so sure that, deep down, he loved her. Groveling had been a big mistake. And here she was, having to grovel to another man. This time to Wyatt Keene—just to pay her bills. What if that proved to be an even *bigger* mistake?

WYATT SAT DOWN ON a bench, his eyes following Casey Sinclair's every move as she took his place on the gym floor. He barely noticed when Mike Granville joined him. Not until the coach murmured, "For someone who looks as if she'd blow away in a stiff wind, she's sure whipping those kids into shape."

"She seems competent enough," Wyatt said with a shrug.

"It helps that she's cute as a kitten."

Wyatt frowned. "I hadn't noticed."

"Really? You've been out of commission too long. I'm a happily married guy, but that doesn't stop me from admiring an attractive woman when I see one."

"The only thing I care about with Ms. Sinclair is her ability to take good photographs."

"That's dandy, Wyatt, because it's *Mrs.* Sinclair." Mike grinned wolfishly as Wyatt gave a visible start. "Yep, that's correct. I heard her tell Dave Welsh, the baseball captain, who was trying to hit on her."

For the first time since the tiny woman with the killer

smile had sashayed into the gymnasium, Wyatt felt the muscles in his neck and shoulders relax. Mike's news-flash made replacing Angela with a vibrant, capable, *married* woman feel like less of a betrayal. The studio was in both their names, but Angela had needed the prestige of owning it. Keene's was tied in to her sense of professional worth, which Wyatt considered sad, since Angela would've made a name for herself no matter where she worked. He would've been content to work out of their home as they had in the early years of their marriage. Angela, who'd come from nothing and grown up an orphan, had needed status, and worked tirelessly to get it. Deep down, she had fears. It was that vulnerable woman Wyatt had fallen in love with. That was the Angela he'd sworn to love and protect. But when she'd needed him most, he'd let her down. He thought it'd be difficult to see another woman in her place at the studio.

Yet life moved on.

He already had Greg Moore, his wife, Brenda, and other friends saying it was time he did—professionally and personally. Today Mike Granville had hinted that Wyatt ought to be open to an attractive woman. Maybe.

His feelings definitely weren't frozen. He'd felt a stirring the minute Casey Sinclair bounded up with her perky attitude. Finding out she was taken, however, made the thought of working with her in Angela's domain a bit easier.

It was better this way. Because these past few months he woke up at least once a night—and often lay there, struggling to conjure up Angela's face. What did that say about him as a husband? Had his love been that shallow? Had his marriage had cracks? Wyatt didn't like any of the answers that popped into his head. All marriages had their ups and downs.

WHEN MIKE HAD TO GO talk to one of the parents who'd come inside to discuss his son, Wyatt was left alone with his troubling memories and his observations of Casey Sinclair.

Listening to her banter, he soon realized she had an easy rapport with the kids, and yet she made clear who was in charge. The careful way she set up her camera reminded him of Angela. Although his wife had always been a bit detached. Even intense. In spite of it her results were stellar; everyone loved her work. People recommended her to their friends, and her reputation spread. Wyatt had been very proud of her.

Would Casey's work reflect a more casual style? Or *was* she casual? Wyatt watched her grow still once she had just the right pose in her viewfinder. Again similar to Angela. Except there was her teasing smile to coax the kids.

It wasn't until Casey dismissed the last of her groups that another remarkable thing struck Wyatt. For at least ten minutes he'd been thinking objectively about Angela without all the guilt that had become second nature to him over the past year.

Letting his chin drop, he flexed his fingers as he stared at the floor. Should he be losing those feelings?

Guilt returned in a rush, and he welcomed its punch. Angela had given so much for her art. She ought to be the one left behind to keep Keene Studio going. Not him.

CASEY HELD HER HEAD high as she approached the sullen man she hoped would give her a job.

"All finished," she said, injecting a chipper note in her voice. She waited until he looked up, gestured them to the other side of the gym where both the swimmers she'd photographed and the baseball jocks were scattering.

Wyatt blinked once, as though clearing away his private thoughts, then rocketed to his feet. "I see you managed that in record time," he said, checking his watch.

"You think I went too fast?" Casey hated sounding defensive, but darn it, that was how he made her feel. "I had a look back at the last few frames," she said, moving in close enough so he could see as she clicked through the final photos she'd taken. "They're pretty good if I do say so myself," she added more confidently.

"I wasn't complaining about your speed." Uncomfortable with how close she'd gotten—he could detect the light, sweet scent of her shampoo—Wyatt raked a jerky hand though his short hair. He dropped to one knee and started fitting his collection of cameras in the black case that sat open on the floor next to him.

Casey cleared her throat. She wasn't sure what to

expect. Was this the whole interview? Would he tell if she was still in the running? Would he pay her for today as promised?

Shifting from foot to foot, she finally blurted, "So what happens now?"

Wyatt slowly lifted his head. "You may go if you like. There's no need to help me pack my equipment." His tone was as cool as the look he bestowed on her.

A faint frown creased her brow. "How should I handle printing the pictures I took? I have an old printer dock at home, but I can't get anywhere near the quality you'll want. Or do you not want these? Was this all a waste of time?"

"No, of course not. I hadn't considered the printing. I guess you'll have to give me your chip. I assume you have a spare. I can off-load the photos and have this wiped clean for you when you come in on Monday to see if there are any assignments."

She popped out the chip and paused before dropping it in his outstretched palm. "I'm confused. Did you just offer me the job? And what do you mean, come in to see if there are any assignments? Your ad made it sound as if you needed a full-time photographer." She paused again. "Coach Granville mentioned that your studio's been closed. For a year, I believe. Does that mean you're starting over, rebuilding your clientele? I'm afraid I need a steady income, Mr. Keene. Being on call won't work for me."

"Please…call me Wyatt. Bear with me if you will. I've never hired an employee before. When I ceased operations, uh, yes, approximately a year ago, Keene Studio was producing at peak. It will naturally take some time to reconnect with clients who've moved on to other studios. Uh…my specialty is sports photography. And animals. I don't know if you've had any reason to look through ranch trade magazines. I did most of those photographs for local ranchers. Weddings, run-of-the-mill family portraits were handled by…" His voice trailed off, and his hands stilled until he hurriedly picked up more equipment, shoving things carelessly into his bag. When he spoke again, his voice was rough. "All domestic photos were done by…someone else."

Casey waited, still unsure what he expected her to say. Was he suggesting that he outsourced weddings and portraits? Hired a freelance photographer? In that case, what exactly was he hiring her to do?

As time dragged on and Wyatt didn't elaborate, Casey felt the need to remind him that she was still there—waiting for clarification. "When I worked at Howell Studios in Dallas, I had a full range of duties. I printed all my own pictures, as well as many shot by the studio owner, Len Howell. He trusted me to choose templates, crop, enlarge, lighten. You name it, I did it."

"Yes, I remember you had a lot of experience, and you came highly recommended. I thought…well, my studio isn't large. Until the business takes off again I don't see any need for us to trip over each other. Not when I can just as easily start out doing most of the computer work myself. Those services you mentioned—cropping, enlarging, touching up—I can do those for now."

"I see. I hope you don't think I'm too pushy if I ask how you intend to make your business take off? Are you sending notices to former clients to let them know you're back at work?"

"I haven't yet, but I suppose I could send out a flyer. Do you really think enough people would pay attention?"

"I had something classier than just a flyer in mind. A beautician I know mailed four-by-six glossy postcards to previous customers when she returned to work at a new salon after having a baby. I did the photo and designed the card. We showed her working on someone at her new station. She said most of her old clients came back."

Wyatt's eyes lit momentarily. "It seems plausible. We...I...have a comprehensive database on everyone who used Keene Studio in the past."

"I'd be happy to help do up a postcard. If you'd like me to, that is."

His nod was slow to come, but just when Casey thought they were making progress, Coach Granville came back and again claimed Wyatt's attention.

CHAPTER TWO

"EXCUSE MY INTRUSION," Mike Granville said to Casey as he placed a hand on Wyatt's shoulder and drew him aside. Wyatt hung back though, and the men stopped to talk only a few feet from Casey. She wasn't trying to eavesdrop, but the coach made no effort to lower his voice.

"I'm assuming we're finished here, Wyatt. Give me five minutes to make sure all the kids have left, and then I'll be in my office. Stop by when you're ready. I'll give you a list of the parents who prepaid for additional copies of the pictures you and Casey took today."

"Sounds good, Mike. I'll be there in a few minutes. Beginning Monday, Casey will be working with me," Wyatt said with a quick glance in her direction. "I'll probably continue to take any future sport photos you need. I thought I should let you know that my studio is going full service again. If you hear of anyone who's looking for a photographer perhaps you could pass that on."

"As a matter of fact, my wife's parents are celebrating their fiftieth wedding anniversary at the end of this month. The other day I overheard Pat and her sister, Anna, making plans for a big blowout. If they haven't booked a photographer yet, I'll have Pat call the studio. Or is it better to drop by your house like I did?"

"Either. I need to get back in the habit of keeping regular studio hours. Or maybe I'll split the in-studio time with Casey," he added, as if in an afterthought.

Still listening, although she'd begun to collect her equipment, Casey couldn't help feeling hopeful. Splitting studio time sounded far more promising than checking in for assignments.

Did that mean Wyatt Keene had had a change of heart? She hoped so.

The men wound down their conversation and Mike went out a back door, presumably to scour the locker rooms for any stragglers. Wyatt walked out on the court and began breaking down his tripods and folding light bars. He acted surprised to find Casey still there when he returned for the case of cameras he'd already packed.

"I thought you'd left. But I guess we didn't set a time on Monday for you to come in. Is ten o'clock too early?"

"Ten is fine." Casey waited, but Wyatt didn't seem inclined to say anything more and turned to go. "I hate to sound crass," she called, "but my understanding was that I'd be paid for helping out with your shoot today."

"That's right!" Wyatt dropped one case with a thump and awkwardly patted his clothing. At last he dragged a crumpled envelope out of his back pocket. "Greg gave me a check before I left his office the other day.

Greg Moore. He's my accountant," he said by way of explanation. "Well, we've been best friends since college." He broke off, looking uneasy, as if he'd shared too much personal information.

"I meant to let you know that in the future Greg will mail your paychecks. So if you move from your current address—not that you will, but if you do—he's the one who needs that information." Wyatt made a halfhearted attempt to smooth the wrinkles from the envelope before handing it to Casey.

"I'll keep that in mind." She glanced down, then back up, into his eyes.

"You know," he said, speaking slowly and deliberately, "it just crossed my mind that instead of driving from Round Rock to Austin every day to see about work, in the beginning, anyway, perhaps you'd rather I called you if I've booked any sittings."

"So, I'm hired, but I wait until you get in touch to say there's a job for me to do?"

"For the time being I think that makes sense, don't you?" He gathered his cases again.

"I'm not sure. How much will I earn?"

"Greg suggested a seventy-thirty split of the fees charged for your jobs. Once we get up to speed and you take on more sittings, we can renegotiate. Is that suitable?" Appearing antsy as he waited for her agreement, Wyatt backed toward the door.

Casey caught up quickly. "I don't know if that will work for me. I need a job that can provide me with steady income from the get-go. This check you gave me today may keep my phone and electricity from being cut off," she said with a nervous laugh, "but it won't pay the mortgage that's due at the end of next week."

Wyatt stopped halfway out the gym door. "That's a joke, right?" He frowned in confusion. "Mike heard you tell one of the students that you're married. What about your husband, Mrs. Sinclair? Is he out of work?"

Casey winced as she stared into Wyatt's dark, suddenly wary eyes. The whole miserable truth about her situation was on the tip of her tongue—every sordid detail about how Dane took off with his frat buddies, leaving her pregnant and dead broke. But she felt a rock wall go up between her and Wyatt Keene, and the words died in her throat before she could speak.

"It *is* Mrs. Sinclair," she managed to mumble. "Please, just call me Casey. And if you don't mind, I'd rather we kept our private lives private."

She tried to ignore the surprise on Wyatt's face, and told herself she hadn't lied—exactly. She *was* technically Mrs. Sinclair. Her divorce wouldn't be final for a few weeks. And if Keene seemed to want her married, so be it. For all she knew, he had a jealous wife at home who demanded that kind of assurance.

She needed this job more than she'd ever needed anything. There'd be time to make a full confession after they'd worked together for a while. After Wyatt saw how competent a photographer she was.

Maybe she didn't seem quite as competent now, with her sweaty hands slipping nervously along her camera and purse straps. Casey chewed the inside of her lip and held her breath. She knew she'd been abrupt, even a little rude, and she wouldn't have blamed him if he'd changed his mind about hiring her.

He didn't do that. In fact, he seemed relieved when he said, "A professional relationship suits me just fine. Tell you what, since money is an issue and I can't afford to lose you over something so simple, I have a plan. Your suggestion of notifying my old customers makes a lot of sense. Go ahead and come into the studio on Monday at ten. I'll have a complete list of former clients ready. I'll pay you to put together and send out the type of postcard you mentioned. Do you have a computer?"

"It's not state of the art, but yes."

"Well, if your equipment can handle it, I guess you can do a postcard at home. It'll save you the gas. I'll have Greg cut a check for supplies. That's the best I can do until orders start rolling in."

"I'll take it," Casey said, grateful she wouldn't have to give up the job before she'd started. Still, the lump in her throat got bigger instead of going away. She hated lying to her new boss—even by ommission. It niggled her into blurting, "I'd never expect to be paid for doing nothing. I promise I'll give you fair work for fair pay."

"I don't doubt it," Wyatt said stiffly as he held the door open wider and motioned for her to pass. After it slammed behind them, he issued terse directions on how to reach Keene Studio.

Casey took in the information, still gripping the envelope with the check. She walked quickly to her car without saying goodbye. She worried that if she didn't get away, she might be sick on his shiny black boots and ruin everything they'd just agreed to.

WYATT STARED AFTER CASEY'S departing figure, and tried not to be concerned about what he was getting into as he loaded his gear into the back of his Subaru Forester. The woman seemed to be a bit odd. But certainly cute, as Mike had pointed out. Which had nothing to do with why he was hiring her. Wyatt couldn't find one thing wrong with how she'd interacted with the kids, or with the glimpse he'd gotten of her pictures. And yet doubts about working with her swirled through his head.

CASEY HAD BARELY CLEARED the parking lot and turned the corner when her nausea made her pull over. She was thankful the clinic nurse had suggested carrying bags with her for the next few weeks in case morning sickness extended into all-day sickness.

Lord, she hoped it wouldn't. If she could manage to survive on a partial wage until Wyatt's business escalated, she might be able to get through the morning sickness without having to face too many clients, she thought as she waited for her nausea to fade, and for the shakes to recede.

Casey knew it wasn't wise to remain parked so close to the school. Her new boss might pass and stop to see what she was doing. She needed a service station with a bathroom. No way could she drive all the way back to Round Rock with this taste in her mouth.

Determined not to worry about what she'd do if this morning sickness kept up, she pulled away from the curb and stopped at the first gas station to appear.

After sponging her face and rinsing her mouth, she actually began to feel human again. Casey found three broken crackers in a plastic bag at the bottom of her purse. She ate the pieces slowly, then couldn't resist, and ripped open the envelope with the check. A hundred dollars. She squeezed her eyes shut with relief. Something to add to Wyatt Keene's plus column—he was generous.

Driving home, Casey allowed her mind to drift back over the day. As well as generosity, Wyatt had everything going for him in the looks department. If he'd been off work because of illness, she couldn't tell. He was robust, tan and all around fit. She'd admired the ripple of muscles when he bent to change filters. From any angle he was attractive.

Not that how he looked mattered. What mattered was if he liked the photos she'd taken today.

Since she was no longer nervous about being interviewed, Casey had time to ponder some of the unanswered questions she had about her new boss. Why had he closed a studio that was producing at its peak? She'd never pry, but she was curious. Or maybe it shouldn't concern her.

But he seemed to jump right on her request to keep

their private lives separate. What did he have to hide? Had he been in jail? The thought burst into her head.

Maybe he'd been in rehab for an addiction of some kind.

Stop jumping to conclusions, she warned herself sternly. In this case, guessing served no purpose. She just needed to dig in and do a good job. She and Wyatt could swap life stories later if they lasted as a team. Her energy would be better spent thinking about what he might say once she had to tell him she was pregnant and would need time off when she had her baby. A boss would have every right to be annoyed with an employee for not mentioning that during an interview.

Casey pressed a hand to her still-flat stomach. She needed time. Time to save money to buy a few baby supplies. And pay for the delivery. At the clinic, her exams were free, but there would be a fee at the hospital. All she could do now was hope for a lot of work and several months to squirrel away some savings.

The only thing for her to do was work hard on each job, and stay out of Wyatt's way as much as possible.

IT WAS AFTER TEN Monday morning before Casey managed to stop throwing up long enough to shower, dress and haul herself out to her car. She felt worse than a cat dragged backward through a knothole. Probably looked like it, too.

Her stomach still felt awful as she drove up the on-ramp to the highway. Her cell phone rang unexpectedly.

She pulled over to the shoulder and fumbled the phone out of her purse. She couldn't imagine who'd be calling. "Hello," she snapped, louder than necessary.

"Casey? It's Wyatt Keene. Where are you? I thought you were going to be here at ten."

"I'm on my way. Traffic," she added hastily. "In the future I'll allow more time for it." She glanced in the rearview mirror and made a face because she realized her tone had been too harsh. "Sorry, I didn't mean to bite your head off," she said, trying to sound pleasant. "I pulled off the road to take your call. I thought maybe it was an emergency."

"No, nothing like that. I don't mean to rush you, but I just got a call from a horse breeder I worked for a couple of years ago. Bill Morrisette. He wants me to come out to his ranch and photograph a horse he plans to advertise at stud. It's quite a drive to his spread—I figure it'll take three hours. I told Bill I'd check with you, then let him know when I'll be there. He needs to groom the stallion—you know, gussy him up for pictures. Take your time. Drive safely. There's no huge rush or anything."

Casey thought about the directions he'd given her to the studio. "I should arrive in twenty minutes. Twenty-five at the most."

"Okay. I have a set of keys to the studio for you. I was wondering…I know we said you'd work on the notices at home…but since Bill phoned here, maybe other clients will, too, given that the number's still in the phone book. If you don't mind holding down the fort, we may pick up a few more jobs even before our notices go out. You'll be paid for the hours, of course."

"Sure, no problem. Will you have a minute to show me how your calendar's set up? I know how we booked appointments at my foster parents' studio, but yours may be different."

"Is that who I spoke with in Dallas? The man who gave you glowing references was your foster parent?"

"If you talked to Len Howell, then yes. He and his wife, Dolly, own the studio. She mostly keeps the books and answers phones. I know it seems sketchy having him vouch for me, but I majored in photography at college. Besides, Len and Dolly wouldn't risk their reputation giving me references I hadn't earned."

"I wasn't criticizing. I— Wow, you're touchy. He did give you high marks, but I judged your work myself. I didn't mean to imply anything negative."

"I am touchy," Casey said hoarsely. "And it's important you don't blame the Howells if I screw up on this job. They're good, decent people."

"Okay, I believe you."

Casey caught a trace of humor in Wyatt's tone. "Um…I'll climb down off my soapbox. If that's all," she said with less force, "I'll get back on the road."

"Right. By the way, I've printed the pictures we took Friday. You'll get a chance to see them before I send them out."

"How are the ones I took?" she asked, holding her breath.

"Good. Great, in fact. Overall, they're better than those I shot of the soccer squads," he said, sounding a little chagrined.

Oops. Casey wasn't sure it was smart to show up her boss right off the boat.

"It's okay," Wyatt added hastily. "Friday was the first time I've touched a camera in ages. It's understandable I'd be rusty."

"I imagine so. Listen, traffic is picking up. If you want to be home from that ranch before dark, I'd better get going."

With a murmured "So long," Wyatt clicked off.

Casey put away her phone, musing again that this man certainly ran hot and cold when it came to conversations. He'd been a whole lot friendlier over the phone than he'd seemed in person.

THE STUDIO, A LOW-ROOFED, brick-and-brown-sided building, sat between two gravel parking areas on a pleasant street lined with green, leafy trees. Casey didn't know what they were, just that they weren't pecans, like those in her front yard. She found the parking strip assigned to Keene Studio and pulled in.

She was prepared to have to knock to get in, but the door was unlocked, and she stepped into a small, but well-appointed waiting room. All four walls held sample photographs. A good variety, Casey thought after a quick appraisal. The smell of photo paper, the beautifully matted and framed prints, reminded her poignantly of Len and Dolly's studio. For the first time since she'd left Dallas to follow Dane, Casey suffered a stab of homesickness so acute it gave her pause.

When she glanced up, she found Wyatt standing in the doorway behind a counter. Over his shoulder she glimpsed familiar signs of a work area. It had been too long since she'd been in one.

To hide her nostalgia, Casey turned back to the wall of photos, all bearing the Keene logo in gold foil. There were portraits of families in various settings. There were several weddings, some formal, others less so. The photographed animals ranged from domestic pets like cats and dogs, to a potbellied pig, a huge yellow snake, and of course, bulls, broodmares and stallions. Casey skipped over several action sports pictures in black and white to study an eleven-by-fourteen photo of a craggy-faced man seated on a tractor. His dog, a brown-and-white spaniel, sat proudly on his lap. "What great detail," Casey murmured in appreciation.

"My father," Wyatt said crisply.

On closer inspection, Casey could see the resemblance. She glanced around at Wyatt, expecting him to say more, but he motioned abruptly for her to follow him into the back room.

She stepped beyond the curtain into a compact work space with all the necessary equipment for a full-service studio.

"Before I take you on the grand tour, here are keys to both doors." He handed them to her, then pointed out desks, computers, printers and racks of software. Wyatt reached through another curtained doorway and snapped on a light in the room beyond. "This space is set up for taking indoor pictures. That's basically it, except for a bathroom down the hall. I told you it was cramped quarters," he said, walking Casey out to the workroom. Stopping at one of the desks, he picked up two manila folders. "I made labels for the families of the kids we took pictures of Friday. The ones who pre-ordered copies. Mike noted the team next to each name. Would you slip the pictures into these envelopes and slap on labels? If you can operate a postage meter, stamp them and take them to the post office. It's on the northeast corner of this street."

"I can do that."

"You listed design experience on your résumé. I found some glossy card stock in the storeroom I think might work for the announcements we discussed. Must've been left over from a holiday open house we held here after we bought this building. Oh, and in this folder are names and addresses of all our old clients."

He frowned so fiercely, Casey didn't dare ask who the *we* might be.

"Is this your appointment calendar?" she asked, moving over to an erasable whiteboard hanging on one wall. The date showing was June of the previous year. Most of the day squares were filled and quite a few seemed double booked. The majority were weddings, but there were other events, too, like bridal showers and birthday parties.

Wyatt stepped between her and the board. He grabbed an eraser hanging from a chain, and with short, angry strokes, cleared the writing. Including the month and year. When everything was gone, he let the eraser fall. "I don't expect you'll have any calls for appointments while I'm gone. If you do, there are paper calendars by each phone. Use those, or leave a note on that desk." He pointed to the smaller of the two desks that sat opposite one another in the middle of the room. "I need to get going. Any questions, jot them down and we'll go over them later. There's no need to stay until I get back. Let me know what time you leave, and check both doors on your way out to be sure they're locked." Grabbing the black bag that sat beside the exit, he left without another word.

She heard the door slam, and let the tension seep from the room before she released her own tightly held breath. "Phew, whatever I did to trigger that, I hope I don't do it again," she muttered. She unconsciously curved one hand over her stomach. It had started to churn as she watched Wyatt obliterate the writing on the calendar.

One thing had been clear from the appointments she'd seen, Keene Studio had been very, very active before it closed down. She wondered once again what had caused Wyatt to take such a long hiatus from a thriving business.

Maybe she ought to ask him outright. Wasn't it natural to be curious? But he'd probably resent her questions. Better just to forget it. Because if she let her mind run wild, heaven knew what expectations she'd come up with.

Instead, she set about taking care of the chores he'd left for her. It was busywork, and that calendar, along with the comments Wyatt had made, bothered her. The collective *we,* for one thing. For another, on Friday he'd said he specialized in animals and sports events, so someone else did the weddings and family portraits.

Ninety-five percent of the appointments on the whiteboard had been weddings. If Wyatt wasn't scheduled to take those pictures, then who was? Especially when he'd specifically said he'd never hired an employee before her.

Something didn't add up. Casey paused in the middle of stuffing the envelopes, and rubbed her temples. Trying to figure out her new boss was too confusing.

She finished labeling the envelopes and gathered them up. On her way out to the post office, she paused in the waiting room.

With Wyatt gone, she was able to make a more leisurely circuit of the display photographs. The bridal shots were some of the best she'd ever seen. In no picture did the background detail detract from the main subject, a mistake too many amateur photographers were prone to make. Couples could pay thousands of dollars to have their special day preserved, only to be disappointed in the results. No, Casey couldn't find a flaw in a single Keene portrait.

Which led her to wonder why the photographer no longer worked with or for Wyatt.

But she wasn't being paid to analyze her employer

or his freelancer. The pictures she'd taken Friday of the swim and baseball teams were excellent, too.

Deciding the mystery might have to remain a mystery, Casey locked the door and ran the stack of envelopes to the post office.

On her way back, she noticed that it was barely two o'clock, so she decided to stay until at least four-thirty or five to start designing an announcement for the studio's reopening.

She hadn't been away from the office more than ten minutes, was surprised to see the phone's message light blinking when she let herself back in.

When she checked, the call turned out to be a hangup. "Shoot, I probably missed the one and only appointment."

What if it'd been Wyatt, checking up on her? After that she could barely concentrate on the announcements. She didn't want him thinking she was slacking off the minute his back was turned. But he'd told her to mail the photos....

As she searched the clip art files for a welcoming image for Wyatt's former clients, she was startled by the phone ringing.

Casey almost fell in her haste to pick up the extension on the other desk.

"Hello," she squeaked. Then, hoping to sound more professional, she added, "Keene Photography Studio."

"Is this Casey Sinclair?" inquired a woman with a soft, melodious voice.

"Yes. Who is this, please?"

"Brenda Moore." Casey didn't recognize the name, so she was grateful when the woman added, "I'm Greg Moore's wife. Greg is Wyatt's best friend and accountant. I bet Wyatt hasn't even mentioned us. Typical." Her laugh was infectious.

"Actually," Casey said, "he did mention you. If you're calling to ask about my tax withholding form, I filled it out and dropped it at the post office today."

"Oh, no. I stay out of Greg's business. I have my hands full at home raising our two-year-old triplets."

Casey's gasp was audible. "Sorry," she said hastily. "I've photographed twins that age. Wiggly, squirmy, each running in a different direction. Three must be hugely challenging. Rewarding, too," she said quickly, not wanting to insult her boss's friend. "I only meant they must keep you busy."

"They certainly do."

With that, Casey heard Brenda cover the receiver and order someone to put down the dinosaur and stop hitting his brother. For several seconds Casey's ears were filled with sounds of stereophonic crying.

"Mrs. Moore. Brenda," she finally said loudly, "Wyatt's not here. He's photographing a horse for a customer and will be gone most of the day. I'll be glad to leave him a message for you. By the way, did you try earlier? I missed a call when I ran to the post office."

"That was probably me. But it's not Wyatt I want. It's you. Greg's birthday is in a few weeks. I thought it would be nice to give him a photo of me with the boys. They're growing so fast. The snapshots we took when they were babies don't even look like them anymore. Would you be able to come to my house this week? The boys will be easier to handle in a familiar place."

"Uh, wouldn't you rather have Wyatt? I mean, since he knows you and your boys."

"Truly? No. Wyatt hasn't popped the cap off a camera since…well, it's been too long. All his friends are delighted he's going back to work. But having a portrait done for Greg's birthday has been on my mind for a while. So when Greg told me Wyatt hired you, I thought it was perfect. Will you come?"

"If Wyatt okays it. This is my first day on the job. Frankly, I'm not sure how much booking Wyatt wants me to do. We haven't really sat down and talked about my duties."

"According to Greg, Wyatt needs all the clients he can get. Greg asked if I'd pass the word among our friends. There are a dozen or so couples who hang out together. We're all University of Texas alumni, so we go back a long time. Of course, our group did include Wyatt and Angela."

"Wyatt and who?"

A low hiss like a slow leak from a punctured balloon came through the receiver. Then silence. After an awkward moment, Brenda sighed in exasperation. "Hasn't Wyatt told you about Angela? Mercy, he had to know her name would come up now that you're taking her place at the studio. Leave it to a man to avoid unpleasant tasks. Listen, tell Wyatt that you're coming to my house tomorrow at ten to photograph Eric,

Emmett, Elliot and me. Is that okay with you, Casey? We'll start with coffee and get to know each other."

"If Wyatt wants me to take the assignment, I will, Brenda. Otherwise…"

"Fiddle-de-dee. It's a paying job, so why would he mind? And promise me you won't sit around stewing about Angela. I swear, men can be so obtuse. Oh, I don't need to tell you. I heard you're married. Yikes, I've gotta run. One of the boys fell, trying to bounce on the couch." Brenda rattled off her address so fast, Casey barely had time to jot it down before the woman hung up.

But all at once her stomach pitched like it had earlier at home before she lost her breakfast. This time she managed to make it to the small bathroom Wyatt had pointed out in his quick tour. She held a wet paper towel to her face until the nausea passed.

Obviously Angela-of-no-last-name had taken those gorgeous photos hanging in the waiting room. It wasn't very nice of Brenda Moore to drop such a bombshell, and then tell Casey not to stew. Who wouldn't? Casey resolved she'd reserve judgment on Brenda. Wyatt had clearly fibbed when he said she was his first employee. Why? Why not admit he was replacing someone?

After that, Casey couldn't focus. She decided she'd do better at home. Dashing off a note informing Wyatt of the appointment, she left both her home and cell numbers and said to call her if he didn't want her going to the Moores'. Then she saved the announcement design she'd worked up to a disk, boxed the card stock, and took Wyatt's list of former customers.

Halfway to Round Rock, she made up her mind that if Wyatt nixed her shoot with Brenda Moore, she'd dig deeper and find out everything there was to know about Angela.

CHAPTER THREE

CASEY MISSED WYATT'S CALL the next morning. She'd gone to the store to replenish her supply of crackers, and he phoned her home number, not her cell. In his message, he sounded okay about her doing Brenda Moore's photos. "Offer her a fifteen percent courtesy discount. I like to do that for friends," he'd said.

It was a kind gesture. Casey hadn't made any friends since she'd been in Texas. Most of the brewpub's customers were guys—not that she'd had time for friendship anyway. Two of Dane's buddies lived in the area and the three of them socialized while she ran the pub. Now she saw how isolated she'd become. It'd be great if she and Brenda Moore hit if off.

She'd worked until 2:00 a.m. finishing the cards for the reopening of Keene Studio. They looked great— bold black lettering on the gilt-edged cards Wyatt had found.

She went to bed confident the notices would go a long way toward rejuvenating Wyatt's business. Unfortunately, sleep evaded her. She tossed and turned and finally got up at five, only to be hit by the worst nausea yet. Crackers didn't help, nor did the ginger ale recommended by the nurse who answered the clinic hotline. When nothing eased her anguish, she cursed her ex-husband. Technically not quite ex. Her court-appointed lawyer said she had to give Dane time to contest the divorce. As if he would. The hard truth was that Dane had never wanted a wife.

Casey still felt ill when it came time to leave for Brenda's. Her stomach protested as she climbed into her car. And why not? All she'd been able to keep down were a few crackers. She tucked a packet of them in her camera bag. If she didn't need them, maybe they'd work to bribe the Moore triplets to sit still and smile.

The nurse on the hotline today had reiterated that morning sickness usually went away by the end of the third month. "Please, Lord, let it be sooner, like today," Casey mumbled as she followed Brenda's directions.

She found the street easily, but a closed gate blocked her path. Brenda hadn't mentioned that she lived in a gated community. Rolling down her window, Casey managed a smile for the guard who stepped out of the security booth. "I'm here to see Brenda Moore."

"Right," the man said as he handed Casey a clipboard to sign. "If you're from Keene Studio, Mrs. Moore is expecting you."

Struck by a fresh wave of nausea, all Casey could do was nod. She was grateful the man took a minute to point out the shortest route so she could recover her composure. Her queasiness had subsided by the time Casey pulled up to a white, two-story home shaded by mature trees and surrounded by a manicured lawn. She parked to one side of a driveway that led to a three-car garage. The Moores might be best buds with Wyatt, but Casey let go of any notion that she and Brenda might become friends. It was obvious they traveled in different spheres.

She grabbed her camera bag and a few props and hurried up the steps to ring the doorbell. Prepared to wait, Casey jumped when the door was quickly thrown open by a harried-looking, slender brunette who held a shy-eyed boy on one hip. The woman grasped the shirt collar of a second tousled child. A third, identical to the other two, clung to her thigh, his big blue eyes glossy with tears.

"Casey Sinclair from Wyatt's studio, I presume?" the woman said. "Please forgive us for being a mess. Believe it or not, we were picture perfect ten minutes ago. Then Elliot dumped two of my newly potted African violets on the living room carpet. Hadley, our old pug, kicked dirt all over the place. The boys had to be bathed again. Plus the dog." Stepping back, Brenda ran a hand through her hair. "I must look a sight by now."

"You look fine." Casey stepped into a high-ceilinged entryway and shifted her equipment to shut the door behind her. She smiled at the boy with the most tears. He peeked at her, then quickly withdrew behind his mother.

"That's Elliot, today's troublemaker. Usually he's the quietest," Brenda said, rolling her eyes. "It's probably a good thing I suggested you and I start with coffee. The boys weren't pleased with a second bath, and this way they'll have a few minutes to play and recover from their crying fits. Then they should be in a better mood for picture taking."

"Wow, I hope I don't have three at once. I couldn't manage," Casey blurted.

Brenda arched an eyebrow. "It's a trial at times. Anyway, welcome to an average day at the Moore household zoo." Easing down the boy she held, Brenda introduced him as Emmett. "And this is Eric. Boys, this is Ms. Sinclair. She's going to take our picture for Daddy. But she and I are having coffee first, so you three can play for a bit." She prompted the boys to wave to their guest before shooing them into a room filled with toys.

With the triplets occupied, she led Casey to an alcove where a small wrought-iron table was already set for coffee. A tray of sweet rolls sat in the center. "Take a seat and help yourself to a Danish," Brenda said, pouring a cup of aromatic black coffee and holding it out to Casey.

The strong scent hit Casey like a brick. And the sight of the gooey rolls made her stomach curdle. Clapping a hand over her mouth, she jumped up. "Excuse me," she said, doing her best to stifle a gag. "Please—I need a bathroom."

With concern on her face, Brenda rushed her to a small, well-appointed bath off the entry. She stepped out and pulled the door shut to give Casey privacy.

Never more embarrassed, Casey lost what little was in her stomach. The ordeal lasted only a couple of minutes. After splashing her face with water and patting it dry, she peered sheepishly out the door. "I'm so sorry. You must think I have some nerve coming to your house ill. I promise, I'm fine. Nerves, probably. The coffee was…overpowering. I'll pass on that, I think. But you go ahead. I…have a snack in my camera bag." She knelt and retrieved her crackers.

Brenda's eyes shone with sympathy. "How many months pregnant are you?"

"Oh, no…" Casey lowered her hands and quickly realized she was rubbing her stomach.

"Let me fix you a cup of ginger tea. Ginger works wonders to combat morning sickness." Brenda escorted Casey back to the breakfast nook, where she whisked away the rolls and removed the coffee carafe.

"I—I…" Casey struggled for something to say while watching the wife of her new boss's best friend fill a teakettle. Her pregnancy was so new, she'd assumed she'd have at least a couple of months on the job before anyone—like her boss—needed to know. "No, it's just anxiety, really." She tried again. "This is my first assignment."

"When I introduced the boys I heard you say you hoped you wouldn't have three at once. Besides, I was an ob-gyn nurse for eight years before I quit to have my kids. I've developed a sixth sense for spotting early signs."

Casey sighed. "I, uh, haven't told Wyatt I'm pregnant. I know I should have at the interview, but I was afraid he wouldn't hire me. You've no idea how much I need this job." She pursed her lips. "My husband…oh, this is more difficult than I'd imagined."

The kettle whistled, and soon the spicy scent of ginger filled the room. Frowning slightly, Brenda set steaming mugs on two place mats. Sitting, she motioned for Casey to take the chair opposite. "Is he unemployed? Your husband?" She gently squeezed Casey's hand.

Casey could have resisted anything but genuine sympathy. Her shoulders slumped. "Our divorce is pending. It'll be final in a couple of weeks. I didn't mention that in my interview, either." She angled her chin defiantly. "I wasn't trying to be sneaky. I didn't think that part was relevant. It's just…been a horrid few weeks."

"I'm sure. Do you want to talk about it?"

Casey hesitated, but Brenda coaxed her story out. In some ways, it was a relief to finally confide in someone.

"I can't believe he walked out the same day you announced your pregnancy. What a creep. No wonder you've developed morning sickness."

"I'll understand if you tell Wyatt about this. After all, you three are friends. It'll be obvious, anyway…before long. I suppose it was foolish to hide the truth until I could prove myself and put enough money aside to have my baby. I think I'm being measured against some invisible standard Wyatt's not sharing with me."

"Angela," Brenda said crisply, wrapping both hands

around her mug. "She's the invisible standard, I'm sure. You're not the only one who's held things back. Wyatt has, too."

"Is Angela the one who took the gorgeous pictures in the waiting room? I don't get it, though. At my interview he said I was his first employee."

"Angela was Wyatt's wife and business partner. She was never an employee. They got married right out of university."

"Oh, wow!" This information seemed incredible to Casey.

Brenda held up a hand. "Wait. We need to talk, but let me check on the boys. They're being too quiet."

Casey sat contemplating this new information until she returned.

"Did she, uh, did Angela dump him?" Casey asked. Dane's defection was still raw, so she could easily imagine how upset Wyatt would be if the same thing had happened to him. It would also explain why he hadn't been able to face working for a year.

Brenda grimaced. "Yesterday, I spoke out of turn on the phone, and I felt guilty all night. Wyatt needs to tell you about Angela himself. But I truly doubt he will. And if I were you, I'd want the scoop."

"I do, if it helps me understand him. That's if he even speaks to me again after finding out that I didn't tell him I'm going to have a baby in eight months."

"It's better that you didn't. He probably wouldn't have hired you." Brenda took a deep breath. "Angela didn't leave him. She died last year—and she was pregnant."

"Oh, no! How awful."

"It was very sad. They waited to start a family until Angela thought the studio was solvent. Losing her and the baby together was a double tragedy for Wyatt. All his friends are delighted to see he's getting back to work."

"How did she die?"

Brenda picked up her cup, then set it down. "I should've kept my mouth shut and let Wyatt tell you when he was ready. But if I don't, someone else will think you know, and they'll bring up Angela's name."

"If his old clients know the story, you're probably right. If he has me stay, somebody's bound to mention her, especially if she took their previous photographs."

"Right. Okay, so Wyatt had always wanted a family. Angela…not so much. She was very focused on her career. She once thought she might be pregnant, but it turned out to be a false positive. A group of us women met regularly for lunch and in May last year she told us she wasn't seeing a doctor again. She wanted to do a home test instead. Wyatt was bouncing-off-the-walls happy when that test was positive. He wanted her to cut back her work schedule immediately."

Casey sipped her tea, unconsciously pressing a hand to her stomach. She didn't know what was coming, but it obviously hadn't ended well.

"Wyatt also wanted Angela to see a doctor right away. So did I. They'd still need to confirm the pregnancy and start her prenatal vitamins if nothing else, given how she skipped meals and worked really long hours. But it was almost June, peak wedding season. Angela sometimes had two weddings booked a day. And she could be stubborn. She claimed she felt fine, so she put off making an appointment."

"What happened?" Casey pressed.

"Angela told Wyatt to get off her back, that she'd see the doctor in July. He stopped hounding her, but still offered to adjust his schedule to help her. Angela refused. She insisted they both keep to their respective schedules so they'd have more money to set up a nursery with designer furniture. She had a difficult childhood, so it was a big deal to her to be able to afford the best. And Wyatt would've given her the moon if she'd asked for it."

"I've sensed that about him—that he's generous."

"He definitely is. And he took on more of the in-studio work. By mid-June Angela had lost weight, and was acting really crabby. Wyatt started insisting she see the doctor. To keep him from harping on it, she finally called, but couldn't get in until the next day. About then, we women convinced her to take a couple of hours off and meet us for lunch. She finally relented. But she forgot she had a rural wedding booked. Because the wedding couple planned to arrive at their ceremony in a hay wagon, Angela asked Wyatt to take the job. Wyatt's always been really good at photographing animals and she just wasn't."

"Did she have a car accident on the way to lunch?"

Casey was desperate to finally hear what had happened to her new boss's wife—what had turned him from the caring man Brenda described to the scarred, grumpy one she'd encountered.

"No. Although that might have been more merciful. Wyatt left around ten to drive to Driftwood. Angela met us for lunch at noon, at her favorite restaurant. I should have picked her up, but I went ahead to deck the table out in pink and blue streamers. We'd decided to make it a surprise celebration. The lunch started out well, but before anyone's food came, Angela complained of abdominal cramps. Gracie, another friend, grew concerned enough to phone the OB. The nurse said Angela needed to come in right away. We all wanted to drive her. She said it was probably gas and that we shouldn't interrupt our lunch. Angela had trouble accepting help from anyone—even when she really needed it." Brenda's voice faded, and for a second, she was silent.

Casey reached over and gripped her hand, feeling tears gathering in her own eyes. "Don't go on. It's enough to know it ended terribly."

"Yes. The OB was thirty minutes away. Fifteen minutes after she left us, Angela called 911 saying she was cramping so badly she couldn't drive. Paramedics found her pulled over on the side of the road. It was already too late. She'd suffered an ectopic pregnancy and her fallopian tube had burst. She'd also miscalculated how far along she was. The E.R. doctor said she was nearer twelve weeks than the eight she thought."

"I don't know a lot about ectopic pregnancy. Is that always fatal?"

"No. A lot depends on the time, the fetus size. In Angela's case, she hemorrhaged so severely the doctors couldn't save her."

"Poor Wyatt. I see why he closed the studio. He must've been dealing with an enormous amount of guilt."

"He pulled back from friends and everything. We've all been so worried. He quit going to the studio and wouldn't see any of us. Greg finally barged in to have him sign some checks, and found Wyatt in a remodeling frenzy. Greg's secretary, Mary, had to phone all Wyatt's clients and cancel the bookings. I know he felt guilty for being out of town, but there wasn't anything he could've done…" Brenda's voice trailed off.

"Even so, it makes me feel worse for not telling him about my pregnancy up front. It's going to be a hundred times more difficult to tell him now."

Brenda nodded. "But you know, Casey, you won't start to show for another few months. In any other circumstances, I wouldn't advise keeping something like this a secret, but Wyatt's just opening up again. Would it hurt to keep quiet for a while? At least until you guys get the studio back on its feet."

Casey shrugged. "I guess not. Though at my height, I may show sooner than other women."

"True. I showed really early because I was carrying triplets. I took pains to buy clothes to disguise my baby bump. I still have them packed away. You're welcome to them if you want them. Staying on with Wyatt would give you time to put some money aside—even if you decide to leave once he finds out about the baby."

"That makes sense. And it's kind of you to offer, but there's no way your clothes would fit me. I might be able to alter them, but you may need your maternity clothes again."

"Not a chance. Greg and I decided three kids are plenty. We're not having more. Besides, I'm a fair hand with a sewing machine. I'm trying to think if any of my outfits couldn't be altered. I'm sure they can all be made to fit you."

"So…you think I shouldn't tell Wyatt I'm pregnant even after I start to show? I don't know, that seems deceitful."

Brenda shrugged one shoulder. "You said you need the job, and I know Wyatt needs you. I'm not suggesting you *never* tell him—just wait until he's had a chance to get comfortable working with you. It might not even take too long. You have a really nice, calm demeanor. The perfect fit for Wyatt."

"I need to give this some serious thought, Brenda. And maybe you should withhold judgment on how perfect I am until after I photograph you and the boys."

"Then let's get this show on the road. Are you feeling better? Your stomach, I mean."

"You know…I am. The ginger tea helped. I'll have to buy some on my way home."

"Take some of mine when you go. I've got lots."

"That's so kind." Casey felt relieved after their talk.

She understood Wyatt's gruffness now. Plus, it was good to get a few things off her chest. Casey sensed a rapport developing with Brenda that she hadn't expected. It would be lovely to have someone to confide in."

"Let me go dress the boys in something suitable," Brenda said. "If you help me keep them corralled, I'll change my blouse and run a comb through my hair, and we'll be set for pictures."

"Why don't I take a few candid shots of them playing? I need to check my meter against the lighting anyway, so that'll give you a few minutes to yourself."

"I could hug you. I'll see if I have matching outfits that still fit them, other than the ones they and the dog got dirt all over."

"It might go more smoothly if we include him in the pictures. I find that kids often act calmer around a favorite pet," Casey said as they moved from the kitchen to the living room.

"What a great idea. Hadley was Greg's dog before we got married. Greg would be touched to see him in the photos."

"Then that's what we'll do. Oh, you have a brick fireplace. Great backdrop. I brought some silk squares to drape over your couch. I'll hold off to see what goes with the outfits you pick out. I generally try a variety of backgrounds, but I lean toward natural, subtle textures. We can shoot several and see what suits you."

"So far everything you've mentioned sounds great.

I'll probably want copies of every shot. Goodness knows what I'll do with them all."

"If the boys have grandparents, a nice photo of the kids alone would make a terrific gift."

"Greg's parents live in Florida, and they're always begging for pictures. My mom doesn't live so far off. Just a couple of hours away, in Kerrville, so she sees the boys pretty often. Still, I imagine she'd like a wallet photo to show her bridge group. Oh, and Greg's mother's birthday is the week after his. When will you have these ready for me to look at? I'll need to drop by the studio without Greg knowing."

"Wyatt's probably going to do the finishing work. He said he would until the studio gets busier. I hope that's soon. One of my favorite things about photography is helping clients select the best shots."

"I'll tell Wyatt I want you to help me."

"No, don't. He might think I instigated it."

Brenda left then, and Casey bustled about checking the light. After the triplets and Brenda were ready, she put Hadley in the middle, petting him and made faces to make the boys giggle. "Perfect," she murmured. "Brenda, you're photogenic. I predict your husband and your family will absolutely love these pictures."

"At this rate I'll have to get a loan to pay for all the copies I'm going to want. I hope Wyatt knows what a gem he has in you, Casey. I wouldn't have thought about including the dog in the photos. Details like that are what make you an invaluable partner."

"Employee," Casey hastened to say. "Don't use the

term partner around Wyatt, please. That would surely remind him of Angela, and I wouldn't want him to think I was trying to take her place."

Brenda started to comment, but was interrupted by Casey's cell phone. "It's Wyatt," Casey hissed. "I wonder what he wants."

"Take the call and see," she said drily.

Casey felt her nervous jitters return. "H-Hello," she stuttered.

His voice boomed out through the phone. "Is everything all right at the Moores'?"

"Fine. Why?"

"The note you left said you were meeting Brenda at ten. It's two o'clock now. If you're going to take this long on every appointment, I'll have to adjust our schedule."

He spoke so loudly that Brenda no doubt heard. She grabbed the phone from Casey. "Wyatt, it's Brenda. One of your darling godsons dumped two pots of African violets all over the carpet. The boys and Hadley had a grand old time playing in the dirt just before Casey arrived. No, it wasn't funny. It meant the lot of them needed hosing down and the living room needed vacuuming. So it's our fault the appointment's run late. Don't be chewing out poor Casey. She handled the delay like a pro. We're almost done. But remember, this is a surprise for Greg. I'm buying an eight-by-ten for his office, a bigger one for over our fireplace, and different poses for Greg's folks and my mom—at Casey's suggestion. You're lucky to have found her, Wyatt. She's a keeper."

There was silence, then Casey heard him say, "Tell her to stop by the studio before she goes home."

With a self-satisfied smile, Brenda clicked off and passed Casey the phone. "Under all his growl, Wyatt's sweet. Remember that, if he snaps. But don't let him walk all over you, either."

"I won't," she said, dropping down to fit her equipment back in her camera case. "If I can get past feeling so sorry for him for his loss. And if I can quit feeling guilty over lying to him."

"It's not lying. The way I see it, you're saving him from making the bigger mistake of letting you get away. You know what? Legally, he can't let you go because of your pregnancy. And knowing Wyatt as I do, I honestly don't think he'd do that even if it hurts him to think of Angela when he sees you pregnant."

Casey hugged Brenda. "I'm so glad you were my first assignment. Guilt's been eating me up. You have a gift for putting things into perspective."

"You deserve a break, and Wyatt deserves a chance to get back on his feet," Brenda said, walking her to the door. "If you need me to smack that jerk ex-husband of yours, I'd be happy to."

"I should have listened to my girlfriends. They tried to warn me not to trust him."

"Don't make excuses for the bum. Guys like that aren't entitled to any."

"You're good for my ego. Next time I feel down, do you mind if I call you?"

"Not at all. Hey, why don't I dig out that box of maternity things tomorrow, and we'll set a date to go over them when I come to see my proofs. Out of Wyatt's earshot, of course."

The triplets toddled up and Casey dropped a kiss on each curly head. "I hope I have just one baby, Brenda, and that he or she is as cute and as healthy as your boys."

"Thanks. I forget sometimes how cute they are. Incidents like this morning notwithstanding." She laughed and the women said a final goodbye.

THE JOY CASEY FELT at making her first potential friend carried over, allowing her to sweep into the studio with a new bounce to her step. She set one of four boxes of announcement postcards on the counter. "I finished these last night, but I didn't want to mail them until you had a look," she told Wyatt as he emerged from the back room.

"You got them all done? Weren't there about a thousand clients on that list?"

"Twelve hundred or so."

Wyatt pulled one card from the box. "These look fantastic," he said. "You must have worked all night on them."

"That's the way I am. Once I start a project, I like to see it finished. I probably only worked until midnight. And very likely I would've been up anyway."

"A night owl, huh? Boy, I can relate."

Casey felt her throat go dry. She swallowed hard and glanced away. He had no idea she knew why he spent sleepless nights. It made her feel ten times guiltier for knowing.

Wyatt seemed to have reached his limit for idle chatter. He cleared his throat and returned the card to the box. "Get them in the mail. I have an appointment in half an hour with a professor from the agriculture program at the University of Texas. They've sold the beef the students raised, but apparently have two promising young bulls they'd like to advertise in a stock magazine. It'll take a little while, so I won't be back here today. Please lock up when you leave. Forward any calls to my home. I wrote down how to do that, and left the note on my desk."

"If you're not coming back to the studio, should I print the photos I took for Brenda Moore?"

"I'll do them tomorrow. You probably haven't used my type of digital darkroom software."

"I'll bet I can figure it out. I used quite a few different programs in Dallas. I started working for the Howells when I was in eighth grade. And Len liked the latest, greatest innovations, too. Dolly teased him that they were going broke buying new stuff." Thinking about the Howells sent a ripple of nostalgia through Casey.

Wyatt eyed her speculatively. "You certainly stuck with one job a long time. What made you leave it and move to Round Rock?"

Casey was sorely tempted to spill her guts. But remembering Brenda's advice, she said simply, "I got married." As she expected, Wyatt backed off from remarking on anything personal.

"Okay, uh…" He slapped a hand on the box of announcements. "After you mail these, go ahead and try out the software. But I'd prefer if you experimented on older photos first, not Brenda's. You'll find a folder on the computer desktop labeled Portraits and Weddings."

"All right. Oh, I had an idea for an initiative to go along with the postcards. When I worked for the Howells, we designed and took pictures for engagement announcements that couples would mail out. I don't know if they're big here, but they were wildly popular in Dallas and very profitable for the studio."

"I've never done anything like that. What kind of design did you use?"

"A tri-fold card. Pastel flowers on the cover. A photo of the engaged couple in the center. A love poem on the final third, plus the couple's names and date of their engagement."

"That sounds very mushy."

"They sold like hotcakes. But maybe couples in Dallas are more sentimental. They might not work here."

"Austinites are no different. There are young lovers everywhere," Wyatt said slowly, tugging at his lower lip. "Tell you what. If you put together a sample—take any photo out of our archives—we'll give your idea a whirl. Our second-most profitable enterprise after weddings were grad photos. Since we've missed this year's June brides and grads, these engagement announcements might help bring in some new clients. In fact, if you'll create an ad, I'll run it in Sunday's paper over the next few weeks."

"Sure, I'd be happy to. Len advertised a lot, so I've done that sort of job before. Competition in our area was stiff."

"Keene's grew mostly through word of mouth, but more studios are opening here," Wyatt admitted. He released a breath. "I won't lie. I'd prefer to quit doing weddings altogether. But I'm proud of Keene Studio. We were full service and I won't let that die."

"Oh." Casey didn't know what to say that wouldn't betray her knowledge of Angela's death.

"What I'm trying to get at," he continued, "is that I let Greg twist my arm to hire help, and it appears I made the best choice, Mrs. Sinclair, uh…Casey."

"Thanks," she said, feeling her face flush at his praise. Her smile wobbled. If he thawed out a bit, Wyatt Keene would be a great guy. Brenda claimed he'd supported his wife in everything—the kind of partner Casey imagined having. The kind she'd once thought Dane was. It made her feel melancholy to realize that however different the reasons, her and Wyatt's marriages had both ended badly.

"Is everything all right?" he asked. "You looked miles away for a minute."

She dredged up another smile, but it was harder to hold.

"Oh, wait, I get it," he said, closing his eyes. "Brenda told you about Angela. I should've known she would. They were friends. We all were—are," he stammered. "Those of us left." Fiddling with his watch, he muttered, "It's probably for the best, anyway. Now that you know, there's no reason to mention it again." Wyatt scooped up his camera case, which he'd left near the door, and with a jingle of the bell, he was gone.

Casey planted both elbows on the counter and rubbed her face. As if that could scour away the sympathy she felt for her boss. Straightening, she started organizing the postcards—just doing her job. It wouldn't do to let herself feel too much of anything for Wyatt Keene. It wouldn't do at all.

CHAPTER FOUR

IT HAD BEEN TWO WEEKS since Casey had taken the Moore pictures. Brenda couldn't come to look at them yet because the boys caught back-to-back colds. Business had picked up at the studio, though, and Casey was happily busy. She and Wyatt rarely crossed paths. They communicated through phone messages and scribbled notes stuck to each other's desk blotters.

She'd left printing the Moore photos to him, and he hadn't done them yet. During her off hours, Casey had created an ad, which had run twice and brought in new customers. She still needed to finish a mock-up of the engagement card, but was feeling more settled now that money was coming in. Her share of the profits covered her food, mortgage, gas and utilities. That was all she needed for the moment.

Today her first appointment was at three at a client's home, giving her plenty of time to work on the mock-up. She popped in to the studio early to look for an appropriate photo in Wyatt's archives. He had ten years' worth stored in banks of lateral files along the walls in the prop room. She made her way past the stacks of equipment—tripods, umbrella lights, racks of rolled backdrops—to find what she needed. She skimmed a hand over a footbridge—a prop for indoor family portraits—knowing her objective today was to unearth the right photo.

She leafed through the folders of prints in the first drawer. No appropriate romantic couples. Moving to the next drawer, she wondered if she'd find any old photos of Wyatt's wife. Casey shouldn't be this curious, but she was.

She didn't come across Angela's name on any folders. Odd, because the photographers Casey knew couldn't resist trying out a new lens or camera on themselves or on coworkers. In Wyatt's case, his wife and partner.

Most couples she turned up in the files didn't suit her purposes. Grad photos were too distinct; so were brides and their wedding parties. Keene's had done tons of milestone anniversaries. She sorted through dozens of those shots. The stats on one white-haired couple said they were celebrating seventy-five years of marriage. Casey gazed at their photo. Angela Keene had captured the love flowing between the pair. Their faces were lined, but serene. Casey touched the print with reverence. What an accomplishment, making marriage last a lifetime. It made her sad to recall how quickly hers had disintegrated.

Growing up as she had, without a father, and with a mother who refused to even name him, Casey had created an idealized notion of what made a happy marriage. Len and Dolly had been great surrogates, but even they couldn't make up for the uncertainty and insecurity of her early years. She dreamed of finding her father.

Casey had always hoped her mom would relent and supply her father's name, but Pam Landis had taken her secret to her grave. Worse, Pam's parents had disowned her before Casey was born. Casey had never met her grandparents, and now they would never meet their great-grandchild. What a shame. Children needed the love of extended family.

As she put the photo of the long-married couple back in the file, she took a moment to wonder if Dane had told his folks about their split or their baby—or if he ever would. The Sinclairs were both overbearing and overindulgent when it came to Dane and his sister. Their mother was a well-known Dallas socialite, their father a tycoon. Would they want to be grandparents?

Shaking off these distressing thoughts, Casey left the archives and headed off to one of Austin's parks. Maybe she'd meet some young lovers who fit the look she wanted for her prototype—and who wouldn't mind signing a release to let her use their picture.

Only a few people were in the park. Darn, if Wyatt hadn't left a note saying he was going to the university to take more photos for the agriculture department, she could have gone there to find a couple. No doubt lots of students would be out and about on such a sunny day, but with her luck she'd run into Wyatt. Casey didn't want him to think she'd gone there to see him.

Ah, finally a couple kissing. She got off two shots and would have taken more, but the man glanced up, and gave Casey such a dirty look that she knew he'd never sign a release form.

Worried about wasting time, she hurried back to her car. On the way, she passed a twenty-something duo, walking along, holding hands. Casey snapped several pictures of their joined hands from behind. It might work. A picture hinting at romance and the possibility of an engagement. She liked that.

Rushing back to the studio, she had a better idea. She could use the photo of the kissing couple and play with shading until they were just a silhouette.

She hadn't actually used Wyatt's print program before, the one he acted so touchy about. But his note had said he planned to go straight home from the university. She'd have time to fiddle a bit before her appointment.

Wyatt's program definitely had more features than any she'd used at Len and Dolly's, but luckily, she found the software manual next to his computer. When ready, she plugged in her chip and set to work blanking out any identifying features of the amorous pair from the park. It took a lot of finessing to blur their features and darken them. Oops, too dark. Casey couldn't see their faces enough to distinguish the kiss.

It was time to leave for her appointment. She hated to go before she had the picture the way she wanted it, but couldn't be late.

The family was ready when she got there. The shoot

went well, and lasted only a little over an hour. Casey decided to head to the studio to exchange chips and finish the engagement card.

She let herself in the front door and went straight to work.

Outside, the sun slid out of sight, but Casey barely noticed. Finally, she had the shot exactly right. She also figured out how to print the silhouette directly on the tri-fold card stock. Her index finger was poised over the print key when a dark shadow fell across her keyboard.

Her head jerked up and a frightened cry stuck in her throat momentarily before bursting from her lips. The rolling chair where she sat skidded sideways, hit an electrical cord running across the floor, toppled and dumped her on her rear.

She struggled to get up as Wyatt snapped on the light next to his computer. Hands on his hips, he bellowed, "What do you think you're doing, working so late and in the dark?"

It took a moment for Wyatt's vision to adjust to the light he'd switched on, and to see that Casey sat with her back flattened against the wall, with eyes wide and terrified.

He hurried over and helped her to her feet. "I'm sorry. When I saw someone in here, I thought you were an intruder. I assumed you'd gone home a long time ago." Still holding her by one arm, he tried to straighten the tails of her shirt, which had ridden up around her middle.

She swatted his hands away. "Your note said you were going straight home after your appointment at the college." After glaring at him, she bent and dusted the knees of her pants, then vigorously rubbed her butt.

"Are you hurt?" he asked, his tone now concerned.

"I'm okay. Only my pride is bruised." She pushed past him to check the image on the monitor. "If you made me ruin the print I've been working on for hours, I'm going to be so pissed."

The corners of Wyatt's lips quirked up at her outburst. To hide his smile, he bent his head and pinched the bridge of his nose. "Well, ah, that's plain enough."

Casey righted her chair and scooted it back to the computer. "I've been trying to finish this sample engagement announcement. I came early to check your archives, but didn't find anything but wedding and anniversary photos. So I went to the park to take pictures. I had consent forms, but I doubted this couple would sign one. I decided to alter their picture to make it work."

Wyatt came to stand directly behind her. "You did all that shading and silhouette stuff with my program?" He leaned over her shoulder to get a clearer look at the screen.

Casey felt the warmth from his body seep into her back, but wasn't comforted by it. Instead, she shivered and rubbed her bare arms. Until his heat wrapped around her, she hadn't realized how cold the studio had become.

Oblivious to the way Casey shrank from him, Wyatt

continued talking. "Print me out a copy so I can see how it translates onto paper."

Reacting to the tension she felt at having her boss crowding her, Casey smacked the print button. She almost rolled the chair over his toes in her haste to put space between them.

It finally dawned on Wyatt that he was making her nervous. He was also suddenly aware of the fact that they were alone in the darkened studio— "I—I saw the glow from the computer screen when I drove past on my way home," he stammered. "That's why I stopped."

"You didn't have to sneak up on me. You could've called out."

Her uneasiness and the way she continued to hug herself rattled Wyatt. "For pity's sake, this is my studio. I have a right to be concerned, especially when the back door wasn't even locked. It could've been anyone in here. Your car isn't in the lot."

"I used the front door. And I parked in the animal clinic's lot because I came from that direction." She nervously waved a hand in the air, then crossed her arms again.

"Dammit, will you quit shaking?"

"Sorry, I can't help it. You scared me! I swear I haven't used the back door at all today. Did *you* leave it unlocked?"

"Maybe…" He looked uncertain. "I ran back in for a second memory chip."

"Next time I decide to work here alone, I'll check both doors. Here's your copy," she said, taking the sheet out of the printer. "I should head home. What time is it, anyway?"

He glanced at his watch. "Almost seven o'clock."

"I didn't know it was so late." She reached past him to collect her camera, her purse and a cardigan she'd draped over the back of her chair. "There are two designs. I'll leave you to print the second. It's more generic, but should still work." Shouldering her purse, she circled Wyatt, aiming for the front entrance.

"I'll print the second version and take both of them home for a closer inspection. If you wait a couple of minutes, I'll walk you out to your car. When I came in, it was dark in our lot, so I'm sure where you parked isn't any lighter."

"I'll be fine without an escort. Besides, this hardly seems like a high crime area."

"It's not, but it never hurts to be careful."

"It's not your problem. I'm the one who decided to stay, so I have to accept the risks. I've got no idea what traffic is like at this hour, but if I don't get going I'll find myself falling into bed before I decide what to fix for supper."

Wyatt glanced up from the monitor where he was preparing to print her second draft. "Late as it is, I should offer to buy you dinner. I haven't eaten yet, either."

"I wasn't hinting."

"I didn't think you were. Jeez, woman." He snatched the sheet from the printer and began shutting down his machine. Suddenly he stopped fidgeting, and an anxious look crossed his face.

It appeared to Casey as if Wyatt wished he could take back his offer. Since she'd lost her breakfast, skipped lunch, and was now starving, she felt just ornery enough not to let him wiggle out of his invitation. "You know, I could do with a bite to eat before I hit the highway. Thanks for the offer."

"Uh, I should've thought before I spoke. I'm sure your husband expects you home for dinner."

"No." Casey didn't elaborate, hoping her terse denial would end that line of questioning. Wyatt had inadvertently reminded her that she was expecting her final divorce papers to come in today's mail. A depressing thought. All the more reason to delay going home. Casey knew this was the opportunity to tell Wyatt the truth about her marriage. At least one secret would be out in the open. But who wanted to admit her personal failures to her boss over a meal? Not Casey.

"So, does your husband work nights or something?"

She cast about for something to say, and settled on a version of the truth. "Actually, Dane's off hiking with friends." Which he was. Right after she'd told him they were going to have a baby, he'd informed her that he had no interest in having a family. He said he'd been pressured into marriage by her and his parents, and in the next breath, announced that he and two college friends had made plans to climb Mount Kilimanjaro and other peaks around the world. And he'd left.

"Oh. Then I guess nothing's stopping us from going

out. How about a hamburger?" Wyatt asked, clearly still hoping she'd turn him down.

Casey's stomach objected to the very thought of greasy meat. "I'm not big on hamburgers," she said. "How does breakfast sound? Isn't there a twenty-four-hour breakfast place a few blocks away?"

"It's a waffle place. Works for me. I'll lock up, walk you out, then I'll follow you there in my car."

It wasn't until Casey was halfway there that she wished she hadn't been such a smarty-pants. How dumb was it to risk eating something that would upset her stomach? All she needed was to be sick in front of her boss.

Okay, she thought, searching for and finding a parking spot. She might be able to handle one pancake with butter and no syrup, and a scrambled egg.

She took her time making her way to the restaurant entrance, only to find Wyatt holding the door for her. It was nice that he had gentlemanly qualities.

The hostess led them to a table in the middle of the room after Wyatt firmly requested they not be given a booth.

Great, Casey thought. What if she threw up in front of the whole restaurant?

Wyatt pulled out her chair, and once he took his own seat, promptly buried his nose in the menu.

Casey looked at hers briefly, then set it aside, commenting instead on the folksy, country decor.

"Do you already know what you want?" He was apparently not in the mood for polite conversation.

She nodded and turned to the waitress, who was hovering nearby. "I didn't see one pancake and one scrambled egg listed on your menu."

"À la carte." The woman tapped her pencil tip on Casey's discarded menu.

"Okay, I'll have that and hot tea. Just butter, no syrup on the pancake, please."

"It comes on the side. You, sir? Or do you need more time?"

Wyatt didn't like being caught frowning at Casey. "No, I'm ready. I'll have your short stack, eggs over easy and bacon crisp." He kept his eyes on the waitress scribbling down his order.

Casey shifted, nervously recoiling at the notion of watching him eat bacon. Her stomach had already begun objecting to the aromas wafting around the room. When the waitress grabbed their menus and took off, she folded her hands and searched for a safe topic. "Business has picked up."

"Uh-huh." Wyatt moved the salt and pepper shakers.

"You went to college in Texas?"

"Yeah. UT Longhorns. Hook 'em, Horns." Smiling, he made the sign.

"Did you grow up on a farm? That's a wonderful picture of your dad in the waiting room. He looks very much at home on a tractor."

Wyatt's lips thinned. "*Was* at home. Two days after I took that photo he died of a coronary occlusion no one knew he had. He never saw the picture. He didn't want it taken, anyway," Wyatt said, stacking packets of sweetener.

"I'm sorry. It's a beautiful memento. I lost my mother when I was thirteen. I don't have many pictures of her. You only have to look at your dad in that photo to see how much he loved you."

"Not really. I was a big disappointment to him. He hated that I majored in photography. A sissy field, he said. He wanted me to be a third-generation pumpkin farmer out there in Uvalde."

"You need to take another look at that photograph," Casey said quietly.

One dark eyebrow shot up. "I've been meaning to ship it to my mom. She sold the farm and moved nearer my sister. To be closer to her only grandkids." Wyatt's jaw hardened. As if he regretted following Casey's lead, he began to drum all ten fingers on the table.

She shifted in her seat once again, noting how she kept breaking her own rule about not discussing anything personal. This time she'd glimpsed another side of Wyatt. It made her wonder if he'd tried to be someone he wasn't for Angela. Casey knew what that was like. She'd turned herself inside out for Dane, but it hadn't done her any good.

Fortunately, their food came, sparing them further awkwardness. Casey was affected by the smell of Wyatt's bacon, and the lump that had risen in her throat. Looking at her plate, she considered saying she wasn't hungry, after all. Would Wyatt care if she excused herself? She buttered her pancake and choked down a bite.

Just then his cell phone rang. After setting down his fork, he flipped it open. "Keene," he said, his eyes locked on Casey's face.

"Brenda, hi. I'm not at the studio. Sorry, but I haven't downloaded your photos yet. I waited until I knew you'd be in. I didn't want Greg stopping by and happening upon them. Um, no, I'm not sure what time she'll be in tomorrow. What do you need her for? Oh, are you sure you don't want me to help you choose?" he asked in surprise. When Casey started to get up, he motioned her down again.

She bit her lip and slowly returned to her seat. *Darn, she'd told Brenda not to get involved like this.*

"No, if you'd rather see this through with Casey, that's fine with me. What time did you have in mind for tomorrow? I'll give her the message."

He wrinkled his nose. "No, don't call her at home. She's, uh, right here. I'll put her on." Wyatt shoved the phone into Casey's hand, then hissed, "Please don't tell her where we are. She'll blab to Greg, and they'll make this a bigger deal than it is."

Casey nodded, but nearly dropped the phone when Wyatt's fingers brushed hers. "Brenda?" she squeaked, and sent him a guilty look at her new friend's response.

"It's late. Where are you two? I phoned the studio and no one answered."

"Actually, we're just leaving. We're in the parking lot," Casey said, thinking quickly. She realized Brenda might hear laughter and dishes clanking. So, springing up, she made a beeline for the door.

Brenda seemed to take her at her word. "Since Wyatt's still there, let's firm up a time tomorrow to look at pictures. Now that the boys are healthy again I want to…you know…get together for the clothes," she added in a whisper. "Call me when you get home. Or I'll phone you. Greg's teaching a finance seminar tonight and won't be back until late. I'd almost forgotten how many dresses I'd kept. Most will be really simple to alter. Let's say eleven at the studio. Oh, pass me back to Wyatt. I have some news to share with him."

Casey grimaced. Wyatt had stayed in the restaurant. "Uh, hang on, Brenda. He's just stepped inside." Whirling toward the restaurant, Casey was hugely relieved to see him striding through the front door, casually stuffing his wallet in his back pocket.

Covering the speaker with her thumb, Casey waved it at him. "Here," she murmured, "Brenda has something to tell you. I didn't mean to take off like that—I just didn't want her to hear the restaurant noises and know where we were."

His eyes smoldered as he lifted the phone to his ear. When Casey waved goodbye and started to back away, he shackled her wrist with his free hand and kept her at his side.

"You've been a busy gal for someone with sick kids," Wyatt said. "In just the past two weeks, you've talked Jana, Gracie and Emily into having family portraits done."

Casey was standing too close to Wyatt. His hand on her wrist made her heart pound. She couldn't really hear what Brenda had to say, but guessed it had something to do with her. She was certain of it when Wyatt stared right into her eyes and said in a falsely sweet tone, "I *do* appreciate you spreading the word about how I've hired a great photographer, Bren." His words belied the tension Casey felt rippling off his body in waves.

"I need more time before I jump back in with the old crowd," he added.

This time Casey heard Brenda's admonition. "That old saying about needing to get right back on a horse after a fall is a cliché for a reason. And I think it also applies if you're avoiding friends, don't you?"

"Life's just not the same," Wyatt said.

They were standing under a streetlight, so Casey could clearly see sweat bead on his forehead.

"It will be now that you've got Casey," Brenda said matter-of-factly. "Assign Jana, Em and Gracie's sittings to her."

"That's not fair to her or any of you."

"Why not? We helped you and Angela build your business in the first place and you know it. We spread the word to coworkers and contacts of coworkers and so on, until the studio made a name for itself. Why wouldn't we help you rebuild it now that Angela's gone?"

"Angela had the drive. I would've been content with less."

"Except…you still have the studio. Come on, Wyatt.

You were good at networking at cocktail parties, talking about the historical value of keeping a family album for posterity. Photography's your passion, too. Don't tell me the drive was all Angela's."

"Greg can tell you I nearly decided to rent out the studio instead of coming back. As for socializing like we used to…I can't do that solo."

"Sorry, I have to hang up, Wyatt. I hear one of your godsons fussing. You won't believe how they've grown since you last saw them. If nothing else, put Greg and me down on your social calendar."

Casey knew Brenda had hung up when Wyatt's grip on her wrist loosened.

"I don't know what you wanted me to stay around for, but I need to go," she said, stepping back. "Will you be okay?" Casey didn't like the dullness of his eyes.

Wyatt roused himself, but that haggard expression didn't vanish. "You didn't eat a bite in there," he said accusingly.

"I guess I wasn't as hungry as I thought. But I hate that you paid for food I wasted. Deduct the cost from my next paycheck."

"Don't be ridiculous. Speaking of paychecks—did you hear? Brenda scored you three more sittings. Look, I'm sorry I've placed you in the position of having to deal with my overzealous friends. You can refuse if you'd rather not."

"If they're all like Brenda, it won't be a hardship. I like her. And the boys are as adorable as can be."

"They weren't even walking the last time I saw them."

Casey heard the gloomy tone in Wyatt's voice. She started to touch his arm, then changed her mind. "The first year after my mom died was the worst. I'm sure people have told you the pain will fade. It does, but the length of time varies from person to person."

His head came up and again their eyes met. Casey thought she'd reached him, but seconds after she sensed a softening, his eyes hardened to granite. "The other day you said we shouldn't get into personal matters. We need to stick to that rule."

"I just... Fine," she said, fumbling in her purse for her car keys. "I'll be in at eleven tomorrow to meet with Brenda."

"Okay. It's your call as to when you want to photograph Jana Mitchell, Emily Endress and Gracie Swartz and their families. If you use the studio, mark the calendar with their names. I'll arrange my in-office time around your sittings."

"Why aren't you happier about this? They're *your* friends, Wyatt. Don't you think it's a nice show of support?"

"I can't imagine why they'd want to support me. I haven't been much of a friend to anyone this past year. I know they want it to be like old times, but it's never going to be," he said with finality.

Casey knew his pain would be less raw if he could move on with his life. She also knew no one could force him out of his grief before he was ready. She jingled her keys. "I'm leaving now. I'll tell Brenda that if your other friends really want photos taken I'll do them. If they just want to use me to corner you into being sociable again, then they should count me out. They need to wait for you to come back on your own."

"Tell Brenda it'll be a long wait." Wyatt took Casey's key ring and unlocked her car. Stepping aside, he held the door and handed back the keys. "I can see you don't get it. Six of us guys met in our first year at UT Austin. We all played baseball—Greg, me, Dave Mitchell, Tom Swartz, Wes Bailey, Ian Endress and Alec Torres. One by one we met girls, one-and-only types of girls," he said with a shrug. "I was last, but eventually we all got married and stood up at each other's weddings." He stopped and hauled in a ragged breath.

"I do get it, Wyatt. What I don't get is, if you were all that close, well, aren't you lonely now?"

"No, everything's different now. Before we congregated at one house to watch sports, while our wives went upstairs, we'd all have a barbecue after the game. Now, it'd be five couples and me—the odd man out. They may believe things wouldn't change, but they'll watch what they say. I'd be… Never mind. If any one of them was in my place, they'd see what I mean." His voice grew rougher the more his emotions surfaced. "Don't pity me. That's another thing I didn't—don't want." He started to slam Casey's car door, but she threw out a hand to stop him.

"There's a difference between pity and sympathy. If you don't want people to pity you, stop acting pitiful."

She yanked her door closed and backed out of the parking spot, crunching gravel under her wheels.

As she drove to the freeway, she wondered how her boss would take being lectured by an employee. And she knew, the advice she'd given Wyatt applied to her, too. She'd felt sorry for herself after Dane walked out, but wallowing in pity hadn't changed her situation.

Lecturing Wyatt gave her a wake-up call. If he didn't fire her for mouthing off, she intended to start each day with a new outlook. Len and Dolly used to say a person should face every day with an "attitude of gratitude." It was high time Casey remembered that. In less than eight months, she'd have a baby to love and care for. She had a good job at the moment, and she'd found a friend in Brenda Moore.

Casey did feel sorry for Wyatt. But the fact remained he was the only one who had the power to make his life better.

Later that evening, when Brenda phoned, that was what Casey told her. "I know you and your friends are anxious to help Wyatt through his grief. You need to realize that's a road each person travels alone."

"You're right, Casey. I should've remembered what it was like for my mom when she lost my dad. Nothing cheered her up. At first, she didn't even react to the news that I was pregnant with her first grandchildren. It took a while, but by the time they were born, she was almost her old self."

"When I lost my mother, the couple who ended up fostering me gave me a book on the five stages of grief—denial, anger, bargaining, depression, then acceptance. And they apply to any traumatic change, not just death."

"Oh, Casey. You mean your divorce, don't you? It doesn't sound like you've accepted it yet, either."

"I probably didn't for a long time, but Dane disappointed me too often. I've accepted it now. My divorce decree came. It was waiting in today's mail. Reading it was like closing a door on part of my life. After seeing Wyatt stuck on anger and depression, I'm getting my act together."

"I may buy a copy of this book and see if Greg will give it to Wyatt. We all want our friend back. When you take pictures for Gracie, Emily and Jana, they'll say the same. I can't wait for you to meet the rest of our group, too—Lou Bailey and Kim Torres. We should all do lunch soon. I'll call them tomorrow. With losing Angela, and then Wyatt going AWOL, the rest of us haven't been as faithful about scheduling time together. And it's a shame. We need to put our heads together and figure a way to help Wyatt get back to normal."

Casey heard a note of fervor she felt she needed to squelch. "Brenda, I'm really happy to be your friend. I've missed girl talk since I left Dallas. But let me be clear—to Wyatt I'm only an employee. It'd be a mistake for you or anyone to think I might take Angela's place. It's a bad idea to try and fit me in with all the friends you've had since college."

"I wasn't…" Brenda didn't bother to finish her sentence. "Maybe unconsciously I was trying, Casey.

I cared about Angela, but she wasn't an easy person. More often than not, our group did what she wanted, or we didn't do it at all. I don't know every little thing about you, but I can tell you aren't demanding like that."

Casey laughed, and it felt good to laugh with a friend. "Believe me, I have plenty of other faults you'll discover if we hang out."

"We will. Tomorrow, after you help me pick out the pictures for Greg, you and I will schedule a clothes-fitting frenzy. I'll get Gracie and Jana to bring their sewing machines to my house. As for the other couples, you can meet them in good time."

"That sounds fine. I was afraid I might have hurt your feelings, being so blunt."

"Not at all. You made me see that Wyatt has to work through his grief himself. Still, it can't hurt for all of us who want him back to his old self to come around the studio to encourage him. Oops, I hear Greg's key in the lock." Brenda lowered her voice. "I'll see you tomorrow at the studio, elevenish."

Casey hung up, feeling a bit as if she'd been caught in a cyclone. Because she'd missed supper, she poured herself a bowl of cereal. As she ate, she went back over her conversation with Brenda. She'd convinced her not to get any ideas about Casey taking Angela's place in that long-standing group of Wyatt's friends. Hadn't she?

Well, if not, she had little doubt that Wyatt would set them straight.

CHAPTER FIVE

CASEY WAS RUDELY JERKED from sleep by her alarm. She scrabbled to find the device on her bedside table, resisting consciousness, wanting to hold on to a vivid dream. *Holy catfish!* Bolting upright, she dropped the now silent clock from her shaking hands. Flopping back down on the bed, she let the threads of the dream grab hold of her again. It was a funny sort. Embarrassing.

Her breasts tingled as she remembered what she'd been doing with Wyatt in her subconscious. Slowly her body and mind coalesced. Yes, those were her curtains. Her bed. Her comforter. Why in heaven's name had she been in the middle of a hot, steamy clinch with her boss?

If Casey thought about it, she could still feel his short, dark hair sliding through her fingers.

"Mercy," she yelped, springing out of bed. *Enough.* She ran her hands down her body in an attempt to rid herself of the last lingering thoughts of Wyatt exploring her, way too intimately. Or maybe not *too* intimately, she thought, going in to wrench on the shower. It had been a wonderful dream. And, on a more down-to-earth note, this was the first time in weeks she wasn't suffering from morning sickness.

Under the steaming shower it wasn't difficult to figure out why her mind had taken such an erotic turn last night. She hadn't been touched or held in ages—hadn't felt loved in even longer. She missed being in an intimate relationship. Why shouldn't she want sex? She was twenty-eight years old, and healthy.

But why pick Wyatt? Then again, why not? He was sensitive. Generous. Hardworking. Gorgeous. Face it, he was attractive, she thought, turning off the water and grabbing a towel. And technically, he was available. For someone. Not her, Casey reminded herself sharply as she wrapped her hair in the towel and did her best to scrub away visions of her boss.

She was pregnant with another man's baby, for crying out loud.

Dragging clean jeans and a sleeveless blouse out of her closet, she dressed, telling herself that she ought to be happy to be feeling better. Hallelujah, maybe her life was getting back on track.

Later, after pouring a cup of ginger tea into her travel mug, Casey left the house feeling almost perky.

A half hour later, she pulled into the studio lot. Oh, no, why did Wyatt's Subaru have to be there this morning of all mornings? It was barely nine-fifteen. Most days they only met in passing. And now she'd be forced to face him with last night's dream fresh in her mind. *Yikes*. Casey nervously ran her hands down the sides of her jeans and checked to be sure the snug blouse didn't reveal any bumps she'd rather keep hidden. Although she was still slim, two days ago the clinic nurse had said her waist was half an inch bigger than at her previous visit.

As she cracked open the door, Casey called out, "Hello! It's just me."

Wyatt rolled his chair to one side of his computer, peering around the monitor at her. "You're early. I've barely finished uploading the chip you shot at Brenda's. I haven't really looked at the photos yet."

"That's okay. Don't let me rush you."

Wyatt hadn't moved, but sat staring at her. Casey eyed him warily over her mug. She set her purse on a bookshelf, unsure whether he wanted her to stay, or leave and come back later.

"Did you see the Meyerson chip?" she asked, strolling over. "I put it on your desk with their order form. They're such a nice family. And they put in a large order, my biggest to date. I, uh, promised to deliver their prints. I know we can't do that for everyone, but Liz Meyerson has multiple sclerosis, so she doesn't drive. I'll make the delivery off the clock, Wyatt."

"I know Bob Meyerson. He played ball in our summer league a couple of years. He had to stop to help out at home when Liz was diagnosed. I haven't seen them for a while, but they sent flowers to—" He broke off, then quickly added, "Don't they have three kids?"

"Four. His mother lives with them now. She's one upbeat lady. I liked her a lot."

Wyatt's gaze returned to Casey's face and she

could've sworn he was looking at her lips before he rolled his chair back to his computer. "I'll pay you for the delivery time. It was good of you to make the offer," he said, his voice rough with feeling.

She flushed. "Like I said, it's not something we'll be able to do after we get busier."

Wyatt frowned, lifted his fingers from the keys and glanced her way again. "It makes no sense to get too busy to do a good turn."

Casey didn't know what to make of his comment. Busyness meant they were making enough money to stay in the black. But perhaps he was thinking back to last June's overbooked calendar. Hadn't Brenda suggested that Angela Keene had put in too much overtime? She'd sounded as if Wyatt hadn't noticed. Maybe he had.

"I'll cover the phones while you go through Brenda's photos. She's anxious to pick the pose she wants enlarged for Greg."

"She'll be more anxious once she sees what you took."

Taken aback, Casey stammered, "Excuse me? What's wrong with them? I remember flipping back through the last half-dozen frames before we stopped. I was sure…I mean, I felt confident that I had several shots where everyone looked fine."

"More like they were *all* good ones," Wyatt said with a snort. "You thought I meant they were bad? Not even close. I agreed Brenda would be anxious because I know her. She's never been able to make a decision in her life. She'll be here all day, dillydallying and deciding which to buy. If you want my advice, steer her toward the ones with Hadley. I guarantee those will be Greg's favorite. He loves that mutt. Whose idea was it to include the dog?"

"Uh, mine," Casey admitted, again uncertain of where she stood. "I thought the kids might settle down better having their pet around. Sorry, I know animals are your specialty. I didn't mean to trespass on your territory."

"Don't apologize. It was a good idea. You don't need to consult me about who or what you include in your photo shoots."

"All right. We never discussed what my specific duties will be. At Howell's I made certain decisions because I was…sort of like family," she said with a shrug. "I don't want to overstep my bounds here."

Wyatt paused. "I expect you to work independently, within reason. For instance, if you see we're low on print cartridges, photo paper or things like that, I want you to order more. On the other hand, if you see a five-thousand-dollar camera you think we can't live without, I want you to consult me. Then I'll say no."

Casey's lips twitched. "I hear you," she said, sipping her tea. "That rule applied at Howell's, too. Okay, I'm glad we've got that sorted out." She moved closer to Wyatt and set her mug down on his desk. "I'm ready to take a gander at the Moore photos."

Wyatt brought the first shot up on the screen.

"Oh, aren't those boys precious? Is that Emmett?

No, wait, that's Elliot pulling Hadley's tail. Is he slightly out of focus?" Casey squinted. "You have no idea how tricky it was getting all of them to sit still at once. It was like trying to trap a tornado in a bottle."

Wyatt threw back his head and laughed.

It was the first time Casey had heard him laugh. The smile brought out a dimple in his right cheek that she hadn't seen before. But now she noticed a network of fine lines at the corners of his eyes. So he hadn't always been so grumpy. The spontaneous laughter left him looking a lot more approachable.

"You should do that more often," she blurted.

Wyatt sobered instantly. That engaging dimple winked out and his jaw tensed. He got up quickly and gestured that she should replace him at the computer.

Casey sat, biting her lip, feeling bad that her remark could have such an effect. It was as if the easy moment had never happened.

He pocketed a set of keys lying beside the computer, then grabbed a large manila envelope and his camera bag, giving every indication of leaving.

"If it's not okay to laugh on this job, I don't know if I can stay here," Casey said, staring defiantly at him.

"Whoa…you can laugh all you like.. I don't want you to be unhappy."

"Then why…?" She trailed off in confusion. But apparently that was all he had to say on the matter because he changed the subject abruptly.

"I'm delivering prints to the breeder I told you about in Dripping Springs. Bill's brother-in-law asked if I'd take pictures of his kids with a couple of sheep that won blue ribbons at the county fair, so I'll be gone awhile. By the way, I booked you a job for tomorrow afternoon. Remember Mike Granville, the coach at the high school? You may have heard him say his wife's parents' fiftieth anniversary was coming up. Pat Granville dropped by my house. She apologized for waiting until so late, but the photographer her sister hired canceled, so we get the gig. Here's the address where they're holding the event." He dug a note out of his pocket. "That's it for jobs this week, unless you book some while I'm gone. After you finish with Brenda, go home if you like. I doubt I'll be back to the studio today."

"Do you have a minute before you take off? Would you mind giving me your honest opinion on which of the Moore photos are best?"

"Brenda doesn't want my opinion."

"I don't think she said it like that, Wyatt. She's being nice because I'm new. And that's not even the point. The Moores aren't the only people who'll see these photos—especially if Greg takes one to his office. If we're trying to spread the word about the studio being open again, don't you think it should be the best possible shot?"

Wyatt didn't agree or disagree, but he set down his things and came to hover behind her chair. "I thought the one you took of the four of them and Hadley casually grouped by the fireplace really stood out. I remember thinking it looked like it belonged in a home and family magazine. It's number twelve or so. Then scroll to the twenties. There's a shot where two of the boys are holding Hadley's ears, and the other is pulling his tail. Brenda's not sure if she should smile, or if she needs to rescue the dog. It's a perfect family action shot. The boys' eyes gleam with mischief. If I were Greg, that's the picture I'd want on my desk."

The minute the words left Wyatt's mouth, Casey felt the atmosphere become strained again. Sadly, it couldn't be clearer that Wyatt envied Greg his family. Casey felt for him as she scrolled through the photos on her computer. Then, although she'd asked for his critique, her nervous stomach returned with a vengeance.

Twisting the cap off her travel mug, she gulped down the cold tea. "Uh, looks like you pinpointed the two best poses," she said hurriedly. "Thanks. I'll print those up and put them in temporary mats so Brenda can see how they look framed. There's one other I think may appeal to her mother. Where they're posed on the love seat. The triplets look like cherubs and Brenda has a Madonna smile. Wait, I just passed it. Here. Is this a perfect grandmother photo, or what?"

"Something smells spicy." Wyatt sniffed the air.

Casey's fingers tightened on her cup to keep from dropping it. "My tea. Sorry, I'll close it." Her mind raced as she pressed the cap on the mug. Wyatt's nearness brought back images from the dream she'd had last night....

"Actually, it's nice. I should know the scent, but I can't place it."

"It's ginger." Affected by his nearness, she rolled her chair forward. Pulling up another program, she opened the photo file and swept away a few dark shadows, then lightened the area around Brenda's hair.

"Whatever you just did capitalizes on Brenda's best features. You know this software better than I do."

"I love what these programs allow us to do. I'd be happy to show you any of the shortcuts I know," she said, glancing over her shoulder to find him standing way too close. Her breath caught in her throat as she watched him tap a thumb on his lips.

"I…may take you up on the offer," he said, but Casey barely heard him. Her thoughts were too busy imagining how his lips would feel against her neck. It wasn't all that warm in the studio, but she felt a ribbon of sweat slide down between her breasts. She wiped a nervous hand across the hollow of her throat. Wyatt's voice seemed to come from miles away when he said, "I've been out of touch, remember."

"Hmm?" Jerking out of her thoughts, Casey did her best to refocus her attention.

"You clean up a raw photograph ten times faster than me. But you sure get caught up in what you're doing." He smiled wryly. "Did you even hear me accept your offer of a few lessons?"

The new, more playful lilt to Wyatt's voice made Casey stop fiddling with Brenda's picture. A hasty peek eased the nervousness in her poor stomach when she saw him smile again. But the silvery twinkle in his eyes suddenly made her pulse race.

Ignoring it as best she could, she tried again to focus on business. "Once people see your ad, I know appointments will pour in. Everyone's going to want holiday photos. We should post a comprehensive list of fees at the counter and by the phones. Uh, not that I'm trying to butt in to your affairs, Wyatt."

"No, that's good. Butt away." His good humor faded a bit, though. "You've probably noticed I'm having a hard time getting back into the swing of things. Fees were an area I left to…" He pinched the bridge of his nose. "I suppose our fees are a bit outdated. Everything's gone up in a year."

Casey was sorry she'd reminded Wyatt of his wife. "Later today I can call our competition. Get some idea of what others in the area are charging."

"I appreciate your willingness to help so much, but that's something I need to handle myself. I'll contact the Texas Professional Photographers Association for some information."

He reached around Casey and collected his gear. This time he didn't stop on his way to the back door. "I'll have the new fees by tomorrow," he called over his shoulder. "Tell Brenda we'll finalize her costs then. And if Gracie Swartz and Jana Mitchell book sittings as Brenda indicated, offer them the same courtesy discount. It's the least I can do for old times' sake. *All* I can do. You did tell Brenda about the discount, right?"

"I did, yes. You know, if other former clients—not personal friends, but ones who used Keene's in the past—book with us again, you may want to offer them a lesser, one-time discount. Think about it," she murmured when he paused at the door to consider her suggestion. "Today, I can take messages and tell them you'll call back."

"I trust you, Casey." Wyatt shifted from foot to foot, acting for all the world as if he wanted to say more. But he left without another word.

She found herself expelling her breath. Wyatt gave her compliments, then acted…guilty. Casey knew how guilt felt. Now that she'd glimpsed a few cracks in his armor and seen those few devastating smiles, it was even worse. She hated to think about the day she'd have to face Wyatt and confess her sins of omission.

WYATT STOOD UNDER THE awning outside the studio door, debating whether to go back inside and apologize to Casey for not being more organized. She was certainly competent. But she unnerved him with the way she had of blinking owlishly at him with those huge, hazel eyes. She hadn't really accused him of incompetence. No, it felt more like she was skittish. Nervous of him for some reason.

Had she been like this during her initial interview? Hard to say. It had been rather haphazard, as she'd pointed out today. One thing he'd liked about her that first day was how she'd stood up to him. He hadn't exactly presented his best side then. Or since, if truth be told. He'd have to try harder.

Maybe he should have told her he'd forgotten he had a good side. At the interview and even now he felt guilty for enjoying watching Casey Sinclair work. He felt especially guilty for appreciating her enthusiasm. She'd understand if he told her no one had loved this job more than Angela. And now Angela was gone.

No, he couldn't do that. Angela had been one of a kind. It would be wrong to expect Casey to be a carbon copy. He didn't want her to be. Getting a firmer grip on his camera case, he left the shade of the overhang and felt the sultry air press down on him. He unlocked the Subaru and tossed his bag on the backseat, impatient to crawl in and turn on the AC. Then the clouds lifted briefly to expose a clear sky. As Wyatt stood next to his car, letting the heat escape, his outlook shifted. For the first time since Angela's death, he looked forward to getting on with his work. He'd loved taking pictures since his mother gave him a camera at age ten.

But ever since Angela's death, he'd wrestled with feeling disloyal about reopening the studio, never mind carrying on with his photography.

Casey represented everything Wyatt had lost. So, yes, in the beginning he'd resented her for being vibrant, sassy and capable—for just *being* there, dammit. As they drifted into a routine, he had less resentment but more guilt—because the unthinkable had occurred. He'd noticed Casey as a person, as an accomplished photographer in her own right…and also as a woman. That was the last thing he'd expected. He never thought he'd have to keep reminding himself that she was married.

Wyatt was about to climb behind the wheel when a

big Suburban pulled up next to him. Brenda Moore hopped out. She gave a squeal of delight and engulfed him in a bear hug.

"Wyatt, you have no idea how good it is to see you. Are you coming or going? I'm here to see my photos and to make appointments for Gracie and Jana to have their family portraits done." She linked her arm through his and started dragging him toward the building.

"Hold it. You were very clear about wanting Casey's help, not mine. She's inside waiting for you. I'm on my way to an off-site appointment."

Brenda's face fell. "I never meant I didn't want your opinion, Wyatt. I was just trying to help Casey get more involved in the business. It sounded to me like you were only trusting her with half the job. I like her—and besides, you can't afford to lose her."

Wyatt did laugh at that. "Well, Ms. Nosy Buttinsky, not half an hour ago I told Casey she's free to make business decisions on behalf of Keene Studio. As for the photos she took of you and the boys, they're some of the best work I've seen." He winced, realizing he was including Angela's photos in that statement.

"Casey's efficient," Brenda said. "And she has a good sense of humor. You should've seen her with my kids. A lot of people are overwhelmed by the three of them in one dose. Casey had an instant rapport. You still don't look convinced. You aren't having second thoughts about keeping her on, are you?"

Wyatt tried to maintain a neutral expression. "Drop it, Bren. I'm not going to fire her. Casey captured an elusive spark in all her subjects. Photographers work long and diligently to acquire that ability, and some never do. Casey has the knack."

"Then why are you so grumpy? You should be thrilled to have hired a person who has the knack."

"Angela had it, too," he said defensively.

Brenda squeezed her eyes shut. "Oh, Wyatt. I can't pretend to understand what you've been going through. But I do know that every single one of your friends would've been happy to help you through it if you let us. Isn't hiring Casey and getting the studio up and running what Angela would want? Surely she wouldn't want you to be a hermit."

Wyatt ran a hand through his hair in frustration. He'd forgotten how persistent Brenda could be. "It's a question I've asked myself a million times this past year. Would Angela want me to reopen? How would she feel about me bringing in a stranger to carry on her work?"

"Well, everyone knows she ate, slept and breathed photography. I'm no authority on the hereafter, but isn't it possible that the best way to keep Angela's spirit alive is to carry on with her passion?"

Narrowing his eyes, Wyatt stared hard at his friend. "When did you become so philosophical?"

Brenda shrugged. "I have my moments. Chalk it up to me being so darned happy to see you back in circulation."

"I'm back at *work,*" he stressed. "I meant what I had

Casey tell you last night, Brenda. I don't want to be put on anyone's social calendar."

"Oh, all right." She pouted. "Men's softball is coming up, though. Greg's counting on you as short-stop. Ian Endress is hosting the first player roundup on his boat Saturday at one. He's still moored on Lake Austin. If you say no to a lake breeze when it's so stifling in town, you deserve to suffer." Sliding her jeweled watch around her wrist for easier reading, she swore gently. "Since I have a sitter, I'm meeting Greg for lunch. I'd better go look at those pictures now so I'm not late."

"Saturday is really the first team get-together?"

Brenda had already moved away, but she glanced back. "Greg said he sent you an e-mail. I think he included a game schedule."

"Could be. I haven't checked my e-mail in at least a week. Tell Greg I'll let him know. Who do they have in mind if I opt out?"

"Um, Larry Crabtree."

"No way. Crabtree can't catch worth spit. Besides, he whines and blames his errors on Wes Bailey at second base. Wes will quit if Larry's shortstop."

Brenda kept walking. She disappeared through the door with a wave.

CASEY HEARD THE FRONT bell ring and came into the waiting area to find Brenda. "Hi. I'd about decided you weren't going to make it."

"I've been here awhile. I was talking to Wyatt in the parking lot."

"Oh. I thought he left ages ago to take pictures of some guy's sheep," Casey said, busily setting out a series of matted photos on the counter.

Brenda dropped her oversize handbag in a chair. "I'm feeling pretty smug, if I do say so myself. I think I've got Wyatt almost ready to come to a get-together on the weekend. The guys play softball every summer. Saturday is when they'll organize this year's team."

"I bet Wyatt tells you to forget it. I warned you last night, remember."

"No, no. I was brilliant. Wyatt loves to play ball. He asked who the team would get in his place. I named the one guy no one wants to be stuck with."

Casey stopped arranging the photos. "So, he's going?"

"Maybe. Wow, Casey, these pictures are fabulous." Brenda zeroed in on Casey's favorite—the Madonna and three cherubs. "I have to get this one for my mother. And another for Greg, and one for my sister. This shot of us with Hadley by the fireplace is perfect for Greg's office. And it'll be the best for his parents and his brother. Oh, but I want a copy of all these for the boys' baby albums. And smaller ones, to tuck inside our Christmas cards. Except…" Brenda pursed her lips. "Greg should be in any photo I send with Christmas cards. After his birthday I'll book another sitting for the whole family. We'll leave the Christmas photo till then. Darn…I can't decide."

Casey pulled out an order form, but her mind was stuck on Brenda's mention of baby albums. It made her long to have one for her baby. "I'll check the sizes you need." She separated the two pictures Brenda had indicated from the rest. "Do you want a glossy finish or matte? Wyatt hasn't updated the fees yet, but he should have them ready tonight. Tomorrow one of us will call you with the final price. Oh, and I was supposed to mention, too, that the friends' discount he's giving you will also apply to Jana and Gracie."

"That's so sweet of him. It proves he's not ready to cut himself off completely." Brenda pored over each of the shots time and again, until Casey grew restless.

She was trying to come up with a polite way of speeding the process along when Brenda suddenly changed the subject.

"Do you know what Wyatt said about these pictures?" Brenda jabbed Casey across the counter and grinned. "He said you have a special knack."

"Really?"

"Uh-huh. He said Angela had it, too."

Not knowing what to make of that, Casey didn't react, so Brenda nudged her again. "Don't you get it? Wyatt thinks you're as good a photographer as Angela was. You've got no idea what high praise that is coming from him. He's given you his seal of approval. Isn't that wonderful?"

"I think maybe you're reading too much into this. He was probably trying to get you to stop bugging him about playing softball."

"Pooh. All right, I deserve that. I swear, though, I heard Greg, Ian and Alec talking about Larry Crabtree. It's not like I make a habit of lying."

Casey rolled her eyes. "Weren't you the one who said I should hide my pregnancy from Wyatt?"

"That's different. You were desperate for a job. And it's not really lying…it's just leaving out part of the truth. We women stick together. But I promise on my daddy's grave, Wyatt did compliment your ability. He said you captured a certain spark in us. And he's right. I'm impressed."

Casey blushed. "Okay, but I almost wish you hadn't told me. Now I'll feel even more pressure to compete with Angela." She drew Brenda's attention to the work hanging on the walls. "Everywhere I look are reminders of how good a photographer Angela Keene was."

Brenda tapped the photos on the counter. "These are just as good as hers. Relax. Keep doing what you're doing. Stop worrying and go get a calendar. Jana and Gracie want me to set up appointments for you to shoot their families."

Laughing, Casey rummaged in a drawer for a scheduling calendar. "Be careful where you say that. You sound like you're ordering a hit."

"That's the Dallas in you showing. Austin's just a little ol' country town."

"I can tell you haven't driven in from Round Rock every day. Austin is spreading out. Kidding aside, Brenda, I have a fiftieth anniversary party tomorrow afternoon. That's it for appointments until word gets out that the studio's open again."

"Schedule Gracie at ten tomorrow. Jana wants Friday, ten or eleven if possible. It's not perfect for your morning sickness, but at least you won't have to deal with total strangers."

"My stomach's better today. I've only needed two cups of ginger tea." Casey gathered the prints. "Wyatt said he likes the smell of my tea. I thought he might ask why I wasn't drinking the coffee he makes every morning, but he didn't."

"Wyatt mentioned your tea? That's not good."

"Why not? I thought it was sweet of him to notice."

"True, but if he noticed that, who knows what he'll notice next. It might be hard to keep hiding the truth."

"Well, it's not something I can hide forever." Casey made a face. "I'll try to be careful when I begin to show. Since I'm short, that may be sooner than for someone as tall as you."

"The most important thing right now is to make sure Wyatt never sees that you're nauseated. That would be a red flag. But maybe you're past the worst, since you said it wasn't too bad this morning."

Casey flushed, remembering the dream that may have had something to do with her feeling better. "Let's hope," she finally mumbled.

"Are we set for checking maternity clothes this afternoon? I have to renege on lunch. Greg invited me out. It's rare to have a sitter, so I'm taking advantage. Can you get away and be at my house by two? That's when Jana and Gracie are bringing their sewing machines."

"Hang on. I had a thought that might put a damper on our plans. What if people recognize your clothes? What if I have to photograph a baby and the mother knows I'm wearing maternity clothes? I mean, how many designers sell to stores in this city?"

"I really wouldn't be concerned about that. I knew a half-dozen women at our country club who were pregnant when I was. I can't recall ever running into my clothes on someone else. And this is only temporary, Casey. I predict that the longer Wyatt is out and about, the less grief-stricken he'll be."

Tears filled Casey's eyes as she finally realized the plan might work. "How can I ever thank you enough, Brenda? Maternity clothes cost a fortune. I'm living paycheck to paycheck as it is. I could never have afforded a whole new wardrobe."

"Listen, don't you worry. And not when it comes to things for your baby, either. In our group alone, we have used furniture and outfits for infants coming out our ears. Most of us went overboard on our first babies."

Casey searched for a tissue, but couldn't find one. Brenda dug one out of her purse and passed it to her. "You can't let Wyatt see you crying, either. It's hormones, hon. Angela had awful crying jags in the first few weeks, too."

Casey tossed the tissue into the wastebasket under the counter. "I'm not sure I can pull this off. I'm scared to death of slipping up. There are so many factors I can't possibly control."

"The prize for pulling it off is helping your boss through a bad patch. He will get through it."

"You're right. I have to do it. I may need frequent pep talks, though."

"Count on me. I'll see you at two. Now I've got to get going. I told Greg to order for me, but if I'm not at the restaurant soon, he'll eat his salad *and* mine," Brenda said with a wink.

Casey followed her new friend to the door. "He sounds like a great guy. Dane and his buddies are so superficial. I tried to imagine any of them caring the way Greg cares about Wyatt. Wouldn't happen."

"It's nice to know someone has your back. That's how it is with our group. You'll see what I mean when you meet the others."

IT DIDN'T TAKE LONG FOR Casey to see what Brenda meant when she arrived for the sewing circle that afternoon. The rest of the women were already gathered in Brenda's living room.

Gracie Swartz was plump and jolly. She wore her long red hair in a single braid, and her freckles looked like spatters of rusty paint across her nose. Her first comment to Casey made her laugh: "You have no idea how happy I am to have someone here who's my height. I've heard every short joke ever told. Start thinking of comebacks now. When you're surrounded by willowy types, a girl can develop a complex."

Jana Mitchell, who sat next to Gracie on the sofa, could easily have passed for a model. Her cocoa-brown skin was a shade lighter than her sleek hair. "What really upsets Gracie," Jana said, walking over to greet Casey with a warm handshake. "Is that some of us can eat our way to Houston and back without gaining weight."

"I look at lettuce and gain ten pounds," Gracie complained.

Brenda hauled two big boxes of clothes into the room. She straightened and ran an eye over Casey's still-slender frame. "Putting on weight is a necessary part of pregnancy. But it's something to keep in mind. Wyatt would never say anything, but it might make him wonder."

Jana took the first dress from the box and shook it out. "I doubt Wyatt will notice that about Casey. Yes, our husbands probably do, but luckily, she's only Wyatt's employee, nothing more."

Casey let the chatter flow around her as the three friends began to fit the clothes to her body. She didn't feel very lucky, no matter what Jana thought. All she'd ever wanted was a happy marriage. And here she carried a baby who wouldn't even have a father. They didn't understand what it was like to grow up fatherless.

How she envied these women.

"Ouch," she said, reining in her wayward thoughts when Gracie accidentally poked her with a pin. Casey gave herself a mental shake. She *was* Wyatt's employee. That was all. She wished she could ask Brenda if lustful thoughts were a side effect of pregnancy—like weight gain and tears. But she didn't dare give Wyatt's friends any ideas. Besides, it was clear from the discussion that the women had joined this conspiracy for Wyatt's sake. The consensus seemed to be that the later Wyatt found out about her pregnancy, the less hurt he'd be by the reminder of his own lost baby.

CHAPTER SIX

THE ANNIVERSARY PARTY for Mike Granville's in-laws was being held in a huge covered plaza the family had rented through the city's Parks and Recreation department. Casey squeezed through clutches of people, hunting for the coach. Unfortunately, she was much later than she'd intended. It had taken a while to find parking in the busy Central district. *There.* She spotted the coach in a huddle of men. They were near one of several cash bars set up around the plaza's perimeter. "Mr. Granville. Coach. Hi," she said, sounding a bit breathless as she dashed up to him. "Casey Sinclair, from Keene Studio."

"Ah, that's right. I remember you."

Casey smiled. "I'm ready to get started. Do you have a shot list for me?"

"My wife will have something. She stopped by a minute ago looking for you. Pat," he called to an attractive brunette in her mid-forties. She was busy directing a line of waiters and didn't immediately respond to his summons.

Once the last waiter left to serve guests. Mrs. Granville hurried over, offering up a tired smile.

"Honey," Mike said, "this is Wyatt Keene's assistant, Casey Sinclair. Casey, my wife, Pat. I know she and her sister, Anna, have specific photos they want taken. I'll leave you to discuss particulars," he said, obviously glad to go back to his friends.

"Anna and I planned for a smaller gathering," Pat said wryly. "We made the mistake of telling our mother to invite whomever she liked. So now we have bridge partners, golf buddies, a travel club, a senior's group. You name it, they're here. And Mom wants pictures of virtually everyone. She gave me a list, but I don't know who half these people are. I'll take you over to my parents and they can direct you. My sister and I would like a picture of them cutting the cake. And Mike and Anna's husband will each be giving a toast, so I'd like one of that. Mother asked if we could get candid shots of people seated at tables, too. At last count we had thirty set up."

"Thirty? I'd better get started. How long does the party last?" Casey hitched her camera bag higher on her shoulder and began to scan the guests.

"The informal cocktail part goes until six. They'll cut and serve cake after that, because some older friends may choose to leave before dark. Then there's a buffet dinner while the band sets up for dancing until ten. If you can stay, we'd love some photos of Mom and Dad's anniversary waltz."

Casey belatedly realized she'd forgotten to bring the larger memory chip she'd set out at the studio. She checked the one in her camera. As she feared, it was definitely too small to hold all the photos Pat Granville had mentioned. "I need to call Wyatt to see if he can bring me another digital chip. If you'll introduce me to your folks, I'll start on the candid shots while I wait for him." Casey could only hope that he hadn't already left the studio. They had passed each other as he arrived and Casey drove away.

Pat had difficulty locating her parents, but eventually found them surrounded by well-wishers. She snagged her mother's attention and introduced Casey to the vibrant couple.

Casey jotted notes on a small pad she always kept in her camera bag. "I'll check with you from time to time," she finally told Letty Hart. "We'll assemble family groups shortly before the caterer brings out the cake. Am I right to assume you'll want pictures with your daughters individually? And perhaps another with their spouses?"

Letty turned to her husband. "Does that sound good to you, Joe? The kids and grandkids will all want pictures with us."

The white-haired, nattily dressed man grabbed another glass of wine from the tray of a passing waiter. "Get 'em now," Joe Hart instructed. "Next time the clan gathers will probably be at my funeral. Who'll want pictures of a dead guy?"

His wife smacked his arm. "Pay him no mind," she said to Casey.

As Letty pointed out certain friends they'd like pictures of, Casey made note of their identifying features. As quickly as possible, she excused herself to find a quiet corner and phone Wyatt.

"Oh, good, you're there," she said when he answered the studio phone. "This little soiree of the Granvilles is more like an epic event. They want oodles of pictures and I left my four-gigabyte chip by the computer after I cleaned off the Moore photos. I hate to impose, but could you bring it to me?" She hurriedly gave him the address in case he'd forgotten it.

"Slow down, Casey. I caught about every third word. Repeat, please."

She cupped a hand around her cell, restating her request while trying to block out the chatter and raucous laughter that was growing louder by the minute. Her quiet corner wasn't so quiet, after all. She gave Wyatt a rundown on the list of pictures the family wanted.

"That's a much bigger job than I thought. Pat said it'd be pictures of her parents and a few family members and close friends. I haven't booked an event in a long time. I should've gotten more specifics. Would you like me to bring my camera and help out when I drop off the chip?"

Casey would love his help. But she wasn't sure if accepting the offer would make Wyatt think she couldn't handle her responsibilities. Most weddings demanded more time and patience than this party. However, she hadn't eaten much today, and already the noise and the worry over forgetting the chip were making her light-headed.

As she vacillated, she found herself wondering what Angela Keene would have done.

"Are you still there?" Wyatt shouted in Casey's ear.

"I'm here. But you've put me on the spot, Wyatt. Will you think I'm less capable if I say I'd like your help?" she asked frankly.

"Isn't that a bit paranoid?"

"Probably. Look, suit yourself. Either way, I need the bigger chip."

"I'll be fifteen minutes max. Keep an eye out for me." The phone went dead.

Casey clapped her free hand to her jumpy stomach. Wyatt had that effect on her; she couldn't bring herself to think about why. Normally she loved working with all kinds of people. But with him she was as nervous as a flea on a hot skillet. She needed to get over that pronto if she wanted to keep her job.

She dropped the phone back in her bag and smoothed a hand over the black jersey tunic she wore with dress pants. It was one of many stretchy outfits Brenda and her friends had altered for her. Casey's waistline had expanded again, or so the physician's assistant had said at this morning's appointment. Only a few centimeters, but Casey was still worried. How long could she keep up this charade before Wyatt noticed?

Pushing those thoughts out of her mind, she got so busy trying to take advantage of the dwindling light that she forgot to watch for Wyatt—until he appeared less than a foot away and broke her concentration. She'd been down on one knee shooting a panoramic view of the anniversary couple and their grandchildren. As she finished then tried to stand, her heel caught on a cobblestone.

"Whoops. Careful." He let his camera bag slip off his shoulder as he steadied her. "I've been searching for you for the past five minutes," he said. "You're too short."

"One more picture and I'd have been hunting for you. Hand over the chip." Casey ignored his petty complaint and simply held out her palm.

"Got it right here." Wyatt pulled the chip out of his bag, then started to rezip the pocket.

"Wait. Let me give you the full one. Since you're going to print the pictures, you can be responsible for the chips."

"Why aren't you printing them?"

Casey looked at him in surprise after installing the larger chip. "Wasn't that our deal? I take pictures, you do the rest until orders pick up."

"They're picking up. This morning I booked a wedding shower, a wedding and one home sitting for a generational photograph. Baby, mom, grandmother, great-grandmother. All as a result of the cards you sent out."

Casey clutched Wyatt's arm and did a little dance of joy.

Reacting to her unbridled enthusiasm, he broke into a grin.

Suddenly they both realized the guests' conversations were lagging as they stopped to stare at the two photographers.

"Oops." Casey sobered and tried to focus on business. "I forgot where we were for a minute. We still have a job to do." She turned away to get a shot of the four-tiered cake being wheeled onto the patio.

Wyatt wasn't as willing to douse his high spirits. He left his bag on the floor, and kept his eyes on Casey. "You look different today," he said, following a very thorough study. "Nice."

Casey stopped shooting, not sure what to make of this observation.

Wyatt stuttered over his next words, likely unnerved by her frown. "Not that you haven't l-looked nice before. You have. Today you look better, uh, dressier." He threw up his hands. "I've dug myself into a deeper hole, haven't I?"

Casey didn't want to say a thing that might cause him further reflection. He might suddenly remember seeing Brenda Moore in this outfit during her pregnancy.

"Get your camera," she said. "We need pictures of the couple cutting the cake, and Pat Granville and her sister requested we get shots of their husbands giving the champagne toast."

"Yes, ma'am," Wyatt responded. Taking out his camera, he trailed after Casey as she squeezed through the crowed of guests, securing a prime location with a view of the cake-cutting ceremony.

For the next several minutes they stood shoulder to

shoulder, cameras whirring and clicking. They worked as a team until Mike Granville spotted them. Leaving his family, he clapped Wyatt on the back, and the two began talking sports.

Casey heard Mike say he was glad to hear Wyatt would be back playing ball. She missed Wyatt's response because waiters began moving among the guests, handing out champagne flutes.

"We'll talk more later," Mike said, and left to take his place beside his wife at the cake table.

A waiter offered Wyatt and Casey flutes of bubbly, which Wyatt accepted and Casey declined.

"No champagne?" he asked, loudly enough that the waiter heard him and paused.

"I don't drink when I'm working."

"It's okay. You're with the boss," Wyatt said jovially.

The waiter turned back to Casey, apparently expecting her to change her mind.

With a smile and shake of her head, she sent him on his way. "The highway from Austin to Round Rock is straight, long and boring. Add alcohol, and that's a recipe for an accident," she said at Wyatt's questioning look.

"I doubt a few sips of champagne will do any harm. Not if you're staying until the dance is over at ten."

"Will we have to stay till the end? I thought once we had pictures of the band, and a few good shots of Letty and Joe during the anniversary waltz, that would be it."

"You don't have to stay longer if you'd rather not,

but Mike said we're welcome to share the buffet at seven-thirty."

"That makes sense for you. You and the Granvilles are old friends. I'm just hired help."

"Where did you get that idea?" Wyatt asked, eyeing her quizzically. "I've probably only spoken to Pat Granville about three times. And once was when she booked this appointment. Besides, this party is for her parents—and you've probably spoken to them more than I have."

Casey elbowed Wyatt in the ribcage and motioned toward Mike, who'd held up his glass and was about to speak. She sidled closer and snapped a series of pictures. She assumed the man who gave the second toast must be Pat's brother-in-law. He was more eloquent than Mike, and his words moved Letty Hart to tears.

Casey captured the emotional moment, along with the honored couple's sizzling kiss. As guests clapped and hooted, Joe Hart bowed. Pat rolled her eyes and passed her mother the knife to cut the cake. With that, the party started up again.

Wyatt nudged Casey's arm. "Do you cry when you photograph weddings, too?" he teased.

Turning aside, she wiped her eyes, first on one shoulder, then the other. She started to say she never cried at weddings, but then remembered what Brenda Moore had said about pregnancy, causing a woman's hormones to go wild. Casey didn't know how she might react at future shoots. "Call me sentimental," she eventually said. "I'm sorry if I embarrassed you."

Wyatt realized that most of the guests who'd been standing around them had now joined a line waiting for cake. Late afternoon sun streaked beneath the canopy and glinted off Casey's short golden curls and damp cheeks.

He took a clean tissue from his pocket and brushed away the last traces of her tears.

Casey sprang back, her fingers flying to the cheek his fingers had touched.

Wyatt couldn't believe what he'd done, and had no defense against the thought rocketing through his mind. Wiping away tears was something he would've done for Angela. Except Angela would never have let him.

Ignoring the incident was the best way to handle it. "So, who's next on that list you have?" he asked briskly. He stuffed his tissue back in his pocket and snatched up his and Casey's camera bags.

She wiped her face one last time, just to be sure no wetness remained. "A great-grandchild. Letty and Joe asked for pictures with each of their extended family. I think it's just wonderful that they have such a big family and they all seem so close. I saw their grandson across the plaza a minute ago. Shall we walk around to get there rather than cut through the crowd?" Wyatt gave his consent and followed even as Casey asked a new question.

"You have a sister, don't you? Do you see her much?"

"No, Linda's in California. Besides, she's twelve

years older than me so we've never been all that close," he admitted.

"That's a big age difference. Are you from a second marriage?"

"No. I was a late surprise. Mom used to embarrass the hell out of me. Still does when anyone's around and she calls me her *gift baby.*"

"Oh, but that's nice. Better than calling you a mistake. I remember you saying she moved after your dad died."

"The farm was too much for her, so she sold it and went to Santa Clara, where Linda and her husband are college professors. Mom wanted to spend more time with her grandchildren. She said she'd be too old to play with any kids I might ever have. Seems she got that right," he mumbled. "Listen to me, rattling on again about personal stuff. This is supposed to be off limits."

Casey shrugged. "My fault for being nosy. Talking seemed a way of passing time while we wait for Lefty to finish cutting the cake."

"There's a lot of waiting in event photography. That's probably why I like taking livestock photos. It's usually a pleasant drive out to a ranch. The owner leads his animal out. I snap three or four pictures from a couple of different angles. We shake hands and I'm back on the road. No stress, no fuss."

"Sounds boring to me. I like to coax just the right smile out of a subject. I also like experimenting with backgrounds. Speaking of which…I looked over your storage room. I can't wait to use some of your fabulous holiday props."

"I don't know what's there. That was always Angela's domain."

Casey didn't want to see Wyatt frown again, so she quickly changed the subject. "I know you take pictures of sports teams for schools. Do you go to games and take the action shots, too?"

"I did during college. Then I freelanced from home for a few years after I graduated. I sold sports pictures to newspapers. Angela didn't like the uncertainty attached to freelancing. She wasn't happy about me being gone four or more nights a week, either. Angela wanted a studio for security and a steadier income, but studio equipment's expensive. We had some lean years..." he murmured.

They'd stepped to the outskirts of the throng of invited guests. Wyatt leaned on one of the poles that supported the canopy. A remote expression sent waves of black shadows to already bleak eyes.

Casey stifled a sigh. It seemed no subject having to do with family or work was safe where he was concerned. She was willing, at this point, to lapse into silence. But Wyatt spoke up again. "It was hard for me to give up those sporting events. In a way, she was right, though. The money from portraits and weddings was steadier. After I cut back, I kept busy with all the details of setting up the studio. Once Angela's wedding business took off, I mostly did billing and matting and framing. That does get boring."

"I can mat and frame. And isn't your billing computerized? Seems to me you could freelance again at sports events if you wanted to." She didn't ask what he did with his evenings now, but she wondered. Her own were hard to fill. Even before the separation, Dane had rarely been home. More often than not he was off with his friends. Back then, she'd kept busy at the microbrewery. Now she was too often at loose ends.

"I've been out of the loop too long," Wyatt said. "Being successful in that circuit means knowing players, managers and newspaper editors. I haven't attended a college game in, well, probably three or four years."

"You're playing ball yourself, aren't you?"

Wyatt straightened away from the pole. "Where did you hear that?"

Noticing how affronted he sounded, Casey wasn't about to get Brenda in trouble. "I, uh, didn't you and Mike Granville just discuss it a minute ago?"

"Oh, yeah. It's nothing, really. An amateur league made up of guys under thirty-five. I skipped the kickoff party, but I'll make the games. Most of the guys on our team have been friends a long time. The wives were, too. Even though Angela didn't come to a lot of the events, I felt funny going back."

"They didn't welcome you by yourself?"

"Yeah, they did…" Wyatt bent his head and rubbed his neck.

"Well, then, I guess I don't see the problem. But it's none of my business, anyway. Hey, I see Letty and Joe are ready for the next photo. That's the great-grand-daughter I mentioned. Isn't she a cutie? Excuse me."

Wyatt was slow to react. He supposed someone like Casey, who still had her spouse, couldn't understand how he felt. It was more than being alone in a crowd of couples. He'd first felt it at Angela's funeral. Amid the mourning, Wyatt sensed an uneasiness, a pulling away by all except Greg, Brenda, Tom and Gracie. His loss caused all the friends to face their mortality. He knew he had to give them time to adjust, but he still felt hurt and isolated. He didn't want to be the elephant in the room—a reminder of how quickly life could be snuffed out. Neither did he want them pitying him, trying to fix him up with their single friends. And they would.

He should give Casey a hand instead of standing here lost in his memories.

Casey, though, had everything under control. She didn't need his help. He liked watching how she went about laughing, joking, trying to entice the little girl to smile. Casey hardly looked older than a child herself. The summer humidity and an evening breeze had turned her short blond hair into a halo of soft, cottony corkscrews around her animated face.

Wyatt smiled at her horseplay. She let the camera hang loose around her neck for a few seconds, while she made horns with her fingers on her head. Twice she lunged forward, lightly tickling the child held in her dad's arms. The little one laughed out loud. Like light-ning, Casey raised her camera and clicked away, catching the child's glee in her viewfinder.

That would produce some great pictures, Wyatt knew. The type Angela had been known for. And yet the women had totally different styles. Angela hadn't been touchy-feely. She knew how to pose a subject, but expected the parents to make their child smile. In the studio they kept a box of toys. Wyatt had only ever seen Angela pass a toy to the mom, then step behind the tripod.

He guessed he hadn't even noticed how stiff Angela had been when it came to dealing with little kids. If not for watching Casey, he wouldn't have thought anything of it.

"Wyatt. Hey, sobersides." Casey bounded up, catapulting him out of his reverie.

And he was glad for the interruption, the chance to think about something else. Angela *had* loved him. He needed to believe she'd wanted their child. Her death had been caused by a tragic medical anomaly. It had nothing to do with how hard she'd driven herself to achieve greater success.

"What's up?" Wyatt asked Casey. Night had crept in, and a huge full moon had risen. Casey's short curls looked even softer than before.

"Can you smell the buffet?" she asked. "Letty says we should eat while we can. We have forty-five minutes or so to kill until we can take shots of the band and the dancing."

"I'm for eating. But then I always like a meal I don't have to cook."

"Do you? Cook?"

"Yeah. I'm not gourmet, but I manage to get a whole meal on the table without burning it. Angela had a lot of evening weddings. She'd phone when she was leaving the reception and I'd have dinner ready when she got home. She took care of breakfast and lunch."

"That's a nice arrangement."

"Doesn't your husband cook at all?"

Casey hesitated before saying, "Never. Uh, maybe I should dash back to the studio and upload this first chip. If these aren't great, we'll still have time to circulate and do retakes. I can eat when I get home."

"Relax. It'll be close to midnight when you get to Round Rock. The food is free. Why not drive on a full stomach?"

Casey hesitated because she worried about being queasy in front of Wyatt. But the food smelled delicious, and the odor wasn't affecting her stomach. "You've convinced me. I can come to the studio early tomorrow, and take a look at these pictures before I head to Gracie Swartz's house at ten."

"That'll put you right in the middle of rush-hour traffic. Is Pat in a hurry for the proofs?"

"No. No. They're not sure yet when the family will get together to choose the shots. Joe Hart joked that the next gathering might be at his funeral." At once Casey clapped a hand over her mouth. "God, I'm sorry, Wyatt. That was so thoughtless of me. I…sometimes my mouth speaks without checking with my brain."

"It's okay. It's been a year. Really, don't sweat it. Let's go fill a plate."

Casey wished she could dig a hole to hide in for a while. It wasn't like she couldn't tell that Wyatt had been observing her all evening. She knew he was comparing her to Angela, and had a horrible feeling she wasn't measuring up.

She hung back, and let several people move between her and Wyatt in the buffet line. He filled his plate with a dab of everything. She took a square of layered Jell-O salad, a roll and a cup of punch. Juggling everything, including her camera bag, she wandered to the bandstand.

Wyatt headed toward a row of chairs, but Casey didn't join him. She didn't feel like making conversation after having to live up to the sainted Angela.

The guitar player tipped his cowboy hat, strummed a riff and smiled at her.

She smiled back and set her cup of punch on the bandstand. With one eye on Wyatt, who was looking around for her in confusion, she made small talk with the guitarist. "I'm one of the photographers for this event. I need to get some shots of Mr. and Mrs. Hart's dance. Will my flash disturb you at all?"

The musician moved closer to her on the stage. "No problemo, pretty lady."

Casey suppressed a grimace at his flirtatious tone. "Could you guys play a few bars of the anniversary waltz so I'll recognize it?"

The man picked up his guitar again and knocked out enough of the tune for Casey to nod.

"How about I ask the drummer to give you a drumroll before we start?" the guitarist said with a wink.

"That would be great." She picked up her drink and turned away to go dump her leftovers in the nearest trash can. She bumped smack into Wyatt.

He lifted his plate above her head to avoid dropping it.

"Sorry, I didn't see you there," she said.

"I know. I saved you a seat. When you didn't show up, I came looking for you." He took a last bite of a corn tamale, then tossed his plate in the trash can, too. His napkin followed after he wiped his fingers. "I heard that guy trying to hit on you. Why didn't you just tell him you're married?"

"He wasn't serious."

"I think he was."

"Get real. He's all of what? Eighteen? Twenty? Far too young for me."

"What difference does that make? He thinks you're hot."

"Stop. I'm nothing of the sort." Casey stopped so quickly, Wyatt steadied her with a hand on her waist. She felt sure her face was on fire as she quickly disengaged herself.

"Obviously, you don't see yourself as guys see you. Tonight, in that outfit, well—I already complimented you on it. And…I was watching that guitar player. He was dying to touch your hair to see if it's as soft as it looks."

"Excuse me? I didn't get that at all. Uh, there goes

the first song. We'd better move or we'll get mowed down." Casey adjusted the settings on her camera to account for night shadows. To calm her nerves, she began snapping pictures.

Wyatt moved to the other side of the stage, where he had a clear view of both the horndog musician and Casey. She was too trusting. Did she really not know how attractive she was? For kicks, Wyatt took her picture as she worked. He'd print them and show her exactly what men saw in her. Or not. That would be imprudent.

Six songs into the set, the stage lights dimmed. After a drumroll, Joe and Letty swung out on the floor. Casey and Wyatt both focused on taking pictures until the anniversary waltz ended.

"That's it. I'm done," Casey announced to Wyatt. She started packing her equipment. "If you see the Granvilles, thank them for giving us the job, won't you?"

"After I walk you to your car."

"That's not necessary."

He took her elbow and escorted her along the walkway. Casey felt the warm pressure of his hand on her arm. Did he know he was making her tingle?

They reached her car, and it took only a few seconds to notice that her left front tire was flat.

"Oh, no!" Casey kicked the offending tire. Then she closed her eyes and banged a fist on the hood.

"Hand me your keys. I'll get your spare."

Casey wasn't as surprised as Wyatt to see that the spare, when he muscled it out of the trunk, was also flat.

"Do you have Triple A?" he asked, dusting off his hands before he dug out his cell phone.

"No," she said, sagging against the vehicle, her mind racing.

"I could run you home," Wyatt said, "but it probably makes more sense to have your husband pick you up. Do you guys have a second car? If his spare fits your car, I'll help put it on. You can get yours fixed or replaced in the morning."

"My husband took a hike." Casey said wearily.

"He's still gone? That must be some hike."

"Dane is off climbing mountains in Africa with his college friends. And he's not coming back. At least not to me." She shoved off the car and walked a few steps away. Crossing her arms, she turned to face Wyatt. "I lied to you. My divorce was final last week."

Wyatt, who'd been about to call his own auto club, almost dropped his cell phone.

"It's true," she said, biting her lower lip. "Good old Dane cleaned out our savings and took off with his friends to Tanzania or God knows where. At our interview, you assumed I was married. I wanted...no, I really *needed* the job. It's splitting hairs, but my divorce wasn't final then. And I didn't think it was relevant, so I never corrected you." Casey rummaged in her bag and ripped out the chip from her camera. She shoved it into Wyatt's hand. "Go ahead. Fire me. You know I can't do the job without transportation. Today it's this tire,

tomorrow maybe another will blow. They're all bald."
She ran her hands through her hair. The air around them
practically quivered, she was so upset.

Wyatt stood there, silently gaping at her, but Casey
didn't care. She was tired of having to keep up the
pretense about Dane. One secret was quite enough for
anyone.

CHAPTER SEVEN

"SON OF A...!"

Casey flinched. Wyatt had a right to be angry, but it changed nothing. She still had no idea what to do or how to get home. Just today she'd taken all the money she'd saved so far and paid the first installment of her anticipated hospital bill. In retrospect, she should've used it for a more immediate need, like new tires.

"You don't have to stay," she said. "This is my problem."

"No," Wyatt said, holding up his hands. "It's nine-fifteen at night and this isn't exactly the auto service Mecca of Austin. We need a tow truck ASAP." Opening his phone, he stepped beneath a streetlight that made Casey's pale face seem even more washed out, and placed a call. Hooking a thumb in his belt, he paced while he waited for someone to answer.

To Casey, even as upset as she was, Wyatt seemed more concerned than angry. She had no idea who he was calling. All she could see were dollar signs.

Wyatt quit pacing and circled her car. He stopped to inspect each of her three remaining tires. "These things are beyond threadbare."

"Look, if you'll give me a lift to the highway, I'll hitch a ride to Round Rock with a trucker. Tomorrow, I'll figure out what to do with my car." She didn't know what, but it beat having the both of them standing on a street corner.

"No way am I letting you hitchhike!" Wyatt straightened, then snapped, "Hello, hello," into his phone.

He launched into a conversation Casey could only describe as typical male car-speak about tire size and rim size. Whoever he was talking to obviously had a solution Wyatt liked. He signed off by saying, "Thanks, Roy. See you soon."

"Who was that?" Casey asked. "Listen, this isn't easy for me to admit, but...I got behind on my bills. I can't afford a tow, let alone a tire. I'm broke."

"I left my car on a side street a few blocks away," Wyatt said, ignoring her. "I'll go get it. You stay here in case the tow truck Roy calls comes before I get back. Wait in your car and lock the doors. Here's my auto club card that authorizes a tow. Again, if I'm not back, you go with him. I'll meet you there."

"Where's *there?* I know I should just thank you, but you're not listening, Wyatt. Believe it or not, tires are on my list of things I need to take care of. But I can't afford them. As embarrassing as this is to admit, I have exactly ten dollars and seventy-nine cents in my bank account. I don't have a credit card. Dane removed my name from our joint card and I haven't been able to get my own yet."

"We'll work it out, Casey," Wyatt said quietly. "You

have money coming from last week's jobs and more from tonight."

She started to say she was already budgeted down to the last penny, but the stormy expression in his eyes stopped her.

"If you want to waste time arguing with me, fine. I'll go first and ask whatever possessed you to get on the highway in that death trap?"

Her fingers curled around the straps of her purse and camera bag. "Maybe I haven't made the best decisions. I gambled on the tires holding out until I caught up on some other bills. I lost. But I'm not a charity case, Wyatt. I do…have options."

"I'm guessing they aren't ones you want to consider."

She opened her car door, threw her bags inside and sank onto the driver's seat, leaving her feet planted outside. With a defiant tilt to her chin, she said, "I can phone my foster parents. They'd drive to Round Rock and take me straight back to Dallas in a heartbeat."

"So why didn't you do that when whatsizname left?"

She leaned forward and clasped her hands, focusing on the pavement instead of Wyatt. "Len and Dolly took me in about the time they should've been retiring. They have plans in the works now. I'm not going to mess it up for them. Besides," she added, looking more glum, "if I went back to Dallas, I'd have to face my friends, and try to explain why Dane walked out."

Wyatt gazed down at Casey's head. She acted tough, but was achingly vulnerable. And if anyone understood that feeling, he did. "Let me put the new tires on my credit card. I'll have Greg deduct the cost from your earnings a little at a time."

Casey sat up, looking hopeful but unconvinced. "How little? For how long?" Wyatt was being so nice about this, she knew she couldn't keep working for him once her pregnancy started to show. It would underscore his loss, as Brenda said often enough. Hurt him, when he'd shown Casey nothing but consideration. Sitting here, she couldn't help but wish that she'd met Wyatt before she'd fallen in love with Dane.

"I phoned a friend's brother. He owns a repair shop," Wyatt said. "I know he'll give us a fair price." He saw Casey's shoulders relax. He also saw relief and something he wasn't sure he wanted to acknowledge creep into her wide hazel eyes. Gratitude. But also something more.

Surely she wasn't mistaking his offer as something…personal. That wasn't an option. Yes, she was attractive, but he wasn't ready to move into that area. Anyway, it was difficult to think of her as divorced, not married. For both their sakes, he needed to squelch those ideas. "You and my wife, Angela, had more in common than photography. She grew up in an orphaned kids' group home and was always passed over for adoption. You were lucky your foster family had a studio and taught you the trade. When I met Angela, she was working three part-time jobs in order to pay for college. You're a gifted photographer, too, Casey. If advancing your earnings means you stay with the studio, it makes good business sense. I'd lose valuable time if I had to run another ad and find someone new."

Just as Wyatt intended, the light faded from Casey's eyes. He hoped he hadn't been too blunt. She'd already been hurt by her jerk of a husband. He hated to hurt her again. On the other hand, he'd done this as much for his sake as hers. Too many times this evening, he'd focused on Casey when he should've been thinking about the job at hand.

"Wyatt, I—"

Impatient to escape an emotional thank-you, Wyatt jingled the loose change in his pockets and briskly turned away.

"The tow truck should be here soon," he called as he headed up the street. "You're going to Roy Mitchell's garage on Cameron Road. Roy is Jana Mitchell's brother-in-law. He does all my auto work." Wyatt almost asked Casey if she'd be all right staying alone, but he stopped himself in time. Anyway, it was a damn stupid question to ask a woman who'd been ready to hitchhike home.

"Go. I'll be fine." She sensed his hesitation to leave her. "I appreciate this, Wyatt. I promise I will repay every cent."

With a cool nod, he walked away.

Casey really didn't like being left by herself on a dark street in an area she didn't know. Telling him she'd hitch a ride with a trucker had been pride talking. But she could tell she'd stretched Wyatt's patience. Why else would he bring up Angela? Casey sighed. It was another comparison she could have done without.

She slid fully inside the car and locked the doors. Taking out her cell phone, she decided to call the one person she figured would help her make sense of the situation. "Brenda. It's Casey. Do you have a minute?"

"Sure. The boys are in bed asleep. I'm waiting for Greg to get home from the finance class he teaches at the university. Are you home? How did the anniversary party go?"

"Fine. But you won't believe what happened." She quickly told her friend about having to call Wyatt to bring her a bigger memory chip. And how he'd stayed, helping to take pictures. "He walked me to my car when we finished, Brenda. And of all the bad luck, my car had a flat tire."

Brenda made sympathetic noises.

"I knew my tires were in bad shape," Casey lamented. "I should have stayed calm, but Wyatt told me to call Dane to come pick me up, and I flipped out. Dane bought the stupid car with bald tires. That's what really ticked me off. Then it just popped out of my mouth that Dane had left me. I confessed everything."

"Wow."

"Yeah. I sort of unloaded on Wyatt."

"I can imagine his shock. Oh, Lordy, Lordy. Did you tell him you're pregnant?"

"No. I started to because I had nothing left to lose. I thought Wyatt would fire me. If not for lying, then because I now don't have transportation. How can I go to clients' homes without a car? The fact is, he bent over backward to help me. He's putting the tow truck and repair costs on his credit card. He said we'll negotiate what I pay him out of future earnings."

"Well, well, well. I'd say you're having a positive effect on him, Casey."

"I guess that's why I feel so guilty for not telling him the rest."

"Listen a minute. He reacted the way the old Wyatt would have. With compassion. That proves he's made enough progress that he can focus on something other than his grief. What if you'd told him about your baby and it reminded him of what he lost and set him back? I think it's a good thing you kept quiet. This way you'll both have more time to work through your individual problems."

"I suppose."

"Heaven knows you need that tire fixed. You have to have a car you can rely on after your baby's born, too, Casey."

"Yes, but…when the whole truth comes out, and you know it's going to, Wyatt will know I lied not once, but twice."

"Maybe not. Not all women learn they're pregnant as early as you did. With the upheaval in your life it's plausible you might not realize for another month."

"I'm not sure I should wait any longer. Business is picking up. It might not be fair to Wyatt."

"You've made my point, Casey. The busier the studio

is by the time you get so far along the pregnancy's obvious, the less Wyatt will want to lose you."

"I don't like lying to him, but I'd hate for him to hurt every time he looked at me."

"That makes you a good person. Sometimes good people need to bend their principles a bit to survive. It's not as if being pregnant is going to keep you from doing a fabulous job for him. Isn't that his number-one priority? Getting his business back to where it makes him a decent living again?"

"You're right. And he did say that getting my tires fixed was purely a business decision."

"There you go."

"Thanks, Brenda, I feel a bit better. Oh, I have to hang up. The tow truck's here."

"Great timing. I hear Greg's key in the lock. Are you still taking Gracie's pictures tomorrow?"

"Yes. Ten o'clock."

"Okay. See you then. She and I thought it'd be a great time to work on the dresses that need alterations. A couple are perfect for the holidays. I know that's still months away, but you'll want to look festive." Brenda lowered her voice. "I promise these dresses will conceal so much, you'd have to be rubbing bellies with Wyatt for him to suspect you're anything but in style."

"Holidays? You mean Christmas? Are you crazy? I'll be seven months along by then."

"I know, but two of these dresses are camouflage extraordinaire. Never mind. You'll understand when you see them. Bye."

"Bye," Casey replied absently. She couldn't help being distracted by Brenda's predictions. The possibility of working undetected into her seventh month was beyond her wildest dreams. If she could, and if she was careful with her money, she could conceivably save enough to support herself and the baby for maybe a month after she gave birth. At which point she'd have to decide what to do next.

Telling herself to take things a day at a time, she got out of the car to meet the tow truck driver. He accepted Wyatt's auto club card without question and began filling out forms. Maybe things would be okay, after all. At her latest clinic visit, she remembered telling the nurse that while she'd never in the world wish her baby away, the timing sucked.

The nurse said a lot of mothers-to-be thought that. But when a mother held her baby in her arms for the first time, all those thoughts vanished. Casey admitted that was probably true, but she still wished Dane had been happy about their baby. The way Brenda said Wyatt had been.

THE TOW TRUCK DRIVER wasn't talkative. During the fifteen-minute ride to Roy Mitchell's garage, Casey tried to picture what her baby might look like. During her first visit to the clinic, she'd had to say whether or not she wanted to know the baby's sex, and she'd said no. Besides, didn't all newborns look pretty much the same? She thought back to the babies she'd photographed, and recalled thinking that if the parents hadn't dressed the child in gender-specific clothes, she wouldn't have known which it was.

She hoped for a girl. But would that jinx her if she wished for a specific sex? She had nothing against boys. It would just be easier not to have a miniature Dane around every day. Since thinking about her loser ex-husband wasn't getting her anywhere, Casey was relieved when the tow truck bounced into a graveled lot in front of Mitchell's garage.

"My directions are to leave your car outside the first bay," the driver said, pointing to three wide closed doors. "Is somebody coming to pick you up? Otherwise I can drop you at the motel down the street. Far as I know, Roy opens at 8:00 a.m."

Panic hit Casey like a sledgehammer. It had never crossed her mind that her car wouldn't be ready to drive in a matter of hours.

But Wyatt said he'd be here. Remembering that eased panic enough for her to say, "My boss told me he'd meet me here. I'm sure he'll take me home."

The words had barely left her lips when headlights cut through the darkness. But the vehicle approaching was a big pickup, not Wyatt's SUV.

A tall guy with brick-red hair hopped out. He seemed more interested in Casey's car than in the two people standing around the parking lot. After a few minutes he sauntered over. "I'm Roy Mitchell." He shook hands with the driver, who tore off a sheet from his clipboard, got Roy's signature, then promptly took off.

Roy turned to Casey. "You must be Casey Sinclair. Wyatt promised if I came here and installed new tires on your car, you'd take my daughter Meg's graduation photographs for free this fall. Wyatt's wife took our daughter Becky's two years ago. No offense, but are you as good as Angela?"

Casey was annoyed at facing yet another comparison to Angela, but she'd learned to disguise her feelings in front of difficult clients. "It's hard to judge my own talent. Perhaps you should ask Wyatt, since he's the one who offered my services," she said.

"Huh. I vouch for the work I do. I know there's not another mechanic in town who comes close to my expertise."

Casey wasn't impressed with Roy's attitude. It was probably fortunate for the sake of her car that Wyatt drove in just then, saving her from saying something regrettable and ruining her chances of getting her tire repaired before morning.

Wyatt climbed out of his Subaru, holding a cardboard tray with three steaming cups. "Roy, thanks a million. Sorry I'm late. I detoured past a coffee drive-through. I see you've met Casey. "

"Her car's a piece of junk," Roy announced. "Are you sure you want four top-of-the-line radials like you said on the phone? It's cheaper to do retreads."

"Coffee?" Wyatt passed Roy a cup. He lifted out another for Casey. She started to decline, but he smiled. "I got you mint tea. It was the only herbal they had."

Casey was grateful, but also concerned about what

Roy had just said. "Wyatt, we only talked about replacing the one flat tire."

The mechanic took the lid off his cup and as he drank, glanced from Wyatt to Casey and back.

"I know, but the other tires are bald, too. What's the point of replacing one if another blows tomorrow?"

"What will that cost?"

Roy rolled his eyes. "Wyatt, I'll go open the first bay while you two talk this over. Then if you'll help me with the winch, we'll put this wreck up on the lift and git 'er done."

Roy left and Wyatt let a moment pass. "Sorry about Roy's lack of finesse. He means well, but can be kind of bossy sometimes."

"It seems to me you were pretty high-handed yourself. He said you promised him a free graduation sitting for his younger daughter."

Wyatt lowered his eyes. "Not only a free sitting, a whole graduation package. It's cheap considering this would cost us overtime anyplace else. Even supposing another shop in town would open up this late."

"It's your studio. You can give away the bank if you'd like. But your pal Roy wants a guarantee that the pictures I take of Meg will be as good as those your wife took of their daughter Becky."

That stopped Wyatt in his tracks.

"Sorry, but what if Meg isn't as photogenic as her sister?" Casey continued. "Or what if Roy and his wife don't like the photos for any one of a hundred reasons?"

"I've seen enough of your work to know they'll like

the pictures." Wyatt glanced away, then tacked on a qualifier. "I'd be more worried that your pictures of Meg will outshine those of Becky."

Casey was so shocked she almost crushed her cup of tea. A dozen retorts ran through her mind. She knew she ought to thank Wyatt for his support, but she could see the torment in his eyes. The compliment had cost him. Somehow that made her admire him even more. He was a much better man than Dane.

She had to stop comparing them. Heaven knew she hated it when Wyatt compared her to Angela. It was just that Dane had stomped all over her heart. Now, if she wasn't careful, she'd find herself counting on Wyatt to pick up the pieces and put them back together. Not wise. She knew a day would come when Wyatt wouldn't want to look at her. And it wasn't far away.

"I'll check your price list and see how a grad sitting compares to Roy's final bill. Then you and I will work out a payment schedule for what's left," she said, determined not to give any hint of her thoughts.

Casey marched off, but wept a little inside as she went in to wait. She grieved for Dane, who had no idea what he'd lost. And for Wyatt, who felt his loss only too keenly. And for herself for being in such an impossible situation.

Grieving, wishing, wouldn't change anything.

Casey sipped her tea, curling a protective hand over her belly. So many times, growing up, she had sworn she'd never be in her mother's circumstances. And here she was, struggling financially and about to become a single mom, too.

Casey flipped idly through a magazine. She half listened to the low rumble of the men's voices coming through the large window that separated her from the bay and forced herself to stop dwelling on things she couldn't change.

Next door the men talked softball as Roy pulled the old tires off the rims. Casey heard Wyatt say, "Yeah, I'm playing. But Dave's right—I haven't made it to any of the team's special get-togethers."

Roy disappeared, presumably to get the new tires, and Wyatt glanced around to locate Casey. He sent her a slightly crooked smile that did funny things to her insides.

"It won't be long," he called.

And it wasn't. A minute later, Roy rolled four tires into the bay and Wyatt knelt to check them. "These look good. I know the retreads are cheaper, but are you sure they're safe?"

Roy nodded. "These tires are gonna outlast her car."

"Okay." Wyatt stood. "Hang on. I'll see what Casey says." He headed for the door to the waiting room.

"I heard," she said when he entered. "Dane knew the car was a junker when he bought it. It's not worth sinking much money into. The retreads are fine."

"It's your safety I'm worried about. But, if these get you by, and you're able to put aside the money you would've spent on new ones, maybe you can buy a better car sooner. A newer used car."

"Sure. Have Roy install those." She looked at her watch, and tried to suppress a sigh.

"It's late," Wyatt stated. "I know you still have a long drive home. Speaking of that drive…wouldn't it be cheaper to take an apartment in Austin?"

"It might be, but I'd lose a lot of money if I sold my house now. Dane refinanced the mortgage before he left, so I actually owe the bank more than it's worth now. Besides, his parents gave us the down payment as a wedding gift. I'd hate for them to think I squandered that."

"Yeah…they raised such a fine son," Wyatt drawled.

Casey had no comeback. And none was needed. Very soon Roy had the tires on her car. Wyatt drove it out of the bay and passed her the keys. The touch of his fingers made her stomach tighten. Still, before midnight, she was on her way home.

BEFORE THEY KNEW IT, the studio had embarked on the busiest period Wyatt said he'd ever experienced. July screeched to a humid close. August morphed into September, which flew past in a blur.

Casey thanked her lucky stars that Brenda, Jana and Gracie had convinced her to continue meeting to finish up altering Brenda's old maternity clothes. By mid-October Casey was into her fifth month of pregnancy and had developed a small baby bump. She worried that maybe the baby wasn't growing well when Lucy Maynard, the clinic doctor measured her abdomen twice at her morning appointment.

"Is something wrong?" This had become her greatest fear. She was happy at work. Her morning sickness was long gone. Wyatt was far more relaxed in her presence. On nights he didn't play ball he lingered to discuss new software or techniques. Life was so idyllic, Casey was sure something awful was going to happen to punish her for still hiding her pregnancy from him.

"Everything's just fine. Your baby's heartbeat is strong. There's movement." Dr. Maynard draped her stethoscope around her neck.

"Yes. The first time was amazing." Casey rubbed the spot where she most often felt a kick.

"The baby's staying tight against your backbone. You'll probably keep thickening around your waist, but I doubt you'll ever look really big from the front."

Casey slid off the exam table and quickly got dressed again.

"You're lucky today's fashions are so loose anyway. Half the women out there could be pregnant and no one would ever know. Everything I've seen you wear makes it impossible to tell that you are."

"Good." Casey bit her lip. "I haven't told my boss yet. I've only had the job a few months."

The doctor smiled. "As long as you remain healthy and feel well, there's no reason you can't continue working, Casey."

"Oh, I know that. But it wouldn't be fair to him. His wife died of complications from an ectopic pregnancy. Seeing me pregnant, being around me every day, would be too painful for him. He's been very kind to me,"

Casey said. "I can't pay him back by hurting him, no matter how badly I want to keep my job."

"Sounds like he's a candidate for grief counseling."

"I doubt he sees he has a problem."

The doctor shook her head. "Men are masters at avoiding things they'd rather not deal with. Which reminds me, Casey, you haven't selected a birthing coach yet."

"I thought I had until December or January to choose one."

"You do. But if you have someone in mind I can give you information packets now. One tells coaches what to expect. And there's a list of signs to look for throughout the latter months of the pregnancy. Most moms choose their husband or a close friend."

"Brenda, the friend I'd like to ask, used to be an OB nurse."

"Perfect. Talk to her soon."

"She has triplet toddlers, so her schedule's not always predictable. I'm not sure she can commit to the hours it requires."

"Your classes start in January. You need a coach by then."

"I'll have someone."

Her appointment had run long. Casey knew she was going to be late for her first session of the day—photographing kids in their Halloween costumes. She'd uncovered great props in the storeroom. Giant pumpkins, a big velvet cat for younger kids to hug. And there were more props perfect for Christmas photos.

Wyatt had agreed with Casey's suggestion of seasonal advertising, but he didn't want any part in helping with holiday photos. She supposed that was understandable. This would be his second Christmas without his wife. Naturally, the season would be hard on him.

She had just pulled into the studio lot, noting the absence of Wyatt's vehicle, when her cell phone rang. The caller was Emily Endress. Over the past few months, Casey had met most of Wyatt's old friends. Emily and Kim Torres were the only two women who still didn't know she was pregnant.

"Hi, Emily," she said. "I bet you're calling to book Halloween pictures of your two little cutie-pies."

"Not quite. Listen, I'm calling from the office, and I don't have long. I'm sure you heard the Hill Country Sluggers took first in their league. Ian's put together a celebration barbecue at six tonight at the marina where we dock our boat. Pier C. Why don't you come?"

"That sounds like fun. Will Wyatt be there?" Casey asked. "Last month at the card party Lou and Wes threw, it felt as though Lou was pairing me with Wyatt. He wasn't overjoyed."

"I didn't hear him complain. Anyway, I honestly don't know if Wyatt's coming. It's just casual. Hamburgers on the boat deck. You don't need to bring anything but yourself."

"Okay, if I'm not intruding. I only made it to two games."

"Like that matters. Angela rarely came to the games

at all, but she was still welcome at the parties," Emily said, then added, "Sorry, I don't mean to keep bringing up her name. I hope Wyatt does come. He needs to relax a bit. You, too. Oh, there goes my other line. See you tonight, Casey."

Casey stewed all afternoon. If only Wyatt would check in, she'd ask if he minded her going. It sounded like a good party, but these were his friends first.

He never called. By the time her last appointment left at five, a fussy little boy who hated both the pumpkin and his pirate suit, Casey needed a break. She drove out to the lake with her car window open, loving the feel of the fall breeze whipping her hair around.

She pulled into the parking lot at the same time as Wyatt. Others were already on the boat, and the barbecue was belching smoke. Wyatt tossed his keys from hand to hand and watched Casey get out of her car.

"Not again," she said. "I told Emily not to try to pair us up."

He dropped his keys and had to scoop them up off the gravel. "And she said?"

"She claimed she didn't know if you were coming. But now I wonder... I'll go." Casey turned back to her car.

"Don't be silly. This is a barbecue. There's absolutely no reason for either of us to leave. Let the others think what they want. How was your day?"

"Good. Until the last appointment." She told him how Timmy Bartlett kicked the pumpkin and refused to wear his pirate hat. They were both laughing when they went on board. One of the men handed Wyatt a beer and took him over to the grill.

Brenda passed Casey a can of ginger ale, and hustled her off to join the rest of the women on the upper deck.

"Did you and Wyatt come together?" Jana had been peering over the rail.

"We met in the parking lot quite by accident," Casey assured her.

"You two should carpool and save gas," Gracie pointed out. "In fact, I think you should hang out a lot more away from work. Don't you agree?"

"Shh, not so loud." Casey glanced down at the men to see if Wyatt had overheard. He hadn't. He was busy talking to Greg and Alec Torres, who were recreating a crucial play from their winning game. Greg's beer sloshed out of his can as he swung his arms. Wyatt quickly grabbed a napkin from a stack by the grill and handed it to his friend. Casey followed their byplay, smiling at yet another example of Wyatt's considerate nature. He possessed all of the good qualities Dane lacked. Dane and his friends would've made fun of the one in Greg's shoes.

Casey didn't realize she'd tuned out the women's conversation until Brenda came to stand beside her at the railing. "Are you falling for Wyatt?" she whispered. "You've hardly taken your eyes off him since you got here."

"It's just those hormones you warned me about, Brenda. And he makes me think of the kind of family my baby won't have. Yesterday, I heard from Dane's mother. He finally told her we're divorced, but apparently didn't mention the baby. She thinks I should be more accommodating of his travels."

"Doesn't that beat all? Even if she doesn't know you're pregnant, can't she see it's wrong for him to sell the pub out from under you so he can go backpacking around the world?"

"He might not have told her that part, either. I didn't feel I could trash her son to her, so I didn't say anything."

Brenda squeezed her arm. "You deserve so much better."

"I know what you're thinking, but it's not going to happen. If things were different, and I wasn't going to have Dane's baby, maybe in time Wyatt might get past his grief. But I'm still no Angela."

"He desperately wanted a baby, Casey."

"Yeah. *Their* baby. I know you guys mean well, trying to set us up. You have to stop," she said, fighting back tears. "Yes, I have feelings for him, but it can only lead to heartbreak. Listen, I have to leave."

Casey thrust her drink into Brenda's hand. "Make up some excuse to Emily and Ian, will you?" With that, she hurried off the boat.

LATER, WHEN THE BURGERS were ready, Wyatt looked around for Casey but couldn't see her. "Where's Casey?" he asked Greg. "She's not seasick, is she?"

"She's fine," Greg said. "She left awhile ago."

"She had a bad headache," Brenda said, coming over with a plate in her hand. "Why don't you call her, Wyatt? Make sure she got home okay. It's a long drive to Round Rock." Wyatt shifted his weight and gazed out over the water.

"Uh, maybe. She probably wouldn't like having me hover."

"Casey's not Angela," Brenda reminded him. "Don't forget that, Wyatt."

He didn't respond, but a few minutes later pulled out his phone and went off to find a quiet spot.

CHAPTER EIGHT

CASEY SET ASIDE THE baby album she'd bought the other day and answered her home phone. She was astonished to hear Wyatt on the other end. "Are you all right?" he demanded.

"Fi-fine," she managed to say. "Why?"

"Brenda said you left the barbecue with a headache."

"Oh. Oh! Uh…I'm okay. Better," she added.

"I won't keep you then. Sorry for bothering you."

"It's no bother. Thanks for checking," she said, not surprised to hear him hang up. She held the phone against her breast while she tried to figure out some logical reason for his call. Finally she decided he was just being nice. A concerned boss. A man whose wife had died after feeling vaguely unwell.

Since the Halloween rush had tapered off, Casey found time on Monday to shoot Meg Mitchell's grad photos.

Wyatt printed them off later that week. "This photo in front of the old waterwheel at Roy's farm is really super. Great photography, Casey. I'd like to hang a copy in the waiting room. It's time I put up new samples.

There's too much emphasis on weddings. Our show-room should reflect the variety we currently offer."

Casey stopped weighing and stamping the last of the Halloween photos to mail out. She walked over to see what it was he liked. "Meg is extremely photogenic. All I did was aim and shoot."

"Why do you do that? Sell yourself short whenever anyone compliments you?" He swiveled around on his chair, catching her off guard with his frown. "This week I also printed off extra enlargements of Mandy Axtell's engagement pictures—the ones you took at the lake. And the shot of Brenda with the triplets and Hadley, plus that Halloween picture you got of the cute little redhead in the witch outfit—the one where's she's kissing the stuffed black cat. Those are all excellent examples of your talent. I plan to hang every one as soon as I frame them."

"You're the one who told me how to use outdoor settings properly, Wyatt. If anyone's responsible for how those particular photos turned out it's you."

"It's nice to have a colleague I can collaborate with. Not that Angela didn't get excellent results," he hastily added. "I, ah, just don't think it's right for the studio to continue to capitalize on her work."

Casey knew the minute Wyatt mentioned Angela that he'd end up clenching his jaw, and then he'd shut down.

"It's your studio," she said, going back to her stamping. "Do what you think is best." Wyatt appeared off in a fog and didn't respond.

"I'm leaving," Casey announced after she ran the last envelope through the meter. "I'll mail these on my way to meet Britney Crane about her wedding on December First. This is the third quote I've worked up. Her mother keeps changing her mind, and since she and Mr. Crane are paying for it, she gets final say."

Wyatt roused. "I know Mr. Crane. He's a cheapskate. Tell Mrs. Crane that if you have to make one more trip I'll be adding on a fifteen percent surcharge for travel expenses."

"They'll cancel and go somewhere else. And then they'll tell their friends not to use us."

"That's a risk I'm willing to take. Business is picking up, so we don't need to tolerate this kind of behavior to stay afloat. It's good you're working with them and not me. I probably would've walked away ages ago. Any idea what time you'll wind down?"

Casey glanced at her watch. "My guess is noonish."

"The least I can do is buy you lunch for all your trouble. Call me when you leave the church and I'll run down to the deli. What would you like?"

Casey thought about what the scale had revealed that morning. "A chef salad. See if they'll put Italian dressing on the side."

"Will a salad be enough? You have three afternoon appointments," he said, checking the whiteboard calendar Casey had set up.

"I ate a big breakfast. And chef salads have lots of ham and egg in them. I wasn't even sure I'd have time for lunch, so I really appreciate your offer."

"Lunch is the least I can do when you're making the bulk of our profit."

Casey managed a casual shrug at the door.

It was closer to one o'clock when she was finally able to phone Wyatt. He had lunch waiting for her when she got back to the studio.

There wasn't anything special about the two of them eating at their desks. All the same it felt intimate to her. She had also noticed that Wyatt had framed and hung her work in the waiting room while she was out. And she was even more shocked to see that he'd taken all of Angela's photographs down. Gone, too, was his earlier despondency.

MIDWAY THROUGH NOVEMBER the studio was swamped by calls from Meg Mitchell's classmates, all wanting Casey to take their graduation pictures. Around that time Casey noticed Wyatt made fewer excuses to leave the studio early. He'd even started joking with people who came in for family portraits.

He and Casey now pretty much split appointments fifty-fifty, except for weddings. And as Wyatt had promised the day he hired her, he adjusted her salary to reflect the new division.

When she got her first paycheck after the raise, Casey splurged and agreed to meet Brenda, Jana and Gracie for lunch. She arrived at the café near the university after the others had already been seated. They rose, greeting her with hugs.

"We're so happy you could get away," Brenda said.

"Your name came up at dinner the other night. Greg told me he'd seen Wyatt, who said his business has tripled thanks to you."

"It has." Casey opened her menu. "We rarely leave the studio before nine or ten o'clock at night." She gave her selection to a busy waitress, who'd already taken the others' orders.

"We?" Brenda raised an eyebrow. "Does that mean Wyatt's getting more involved in operations?"

"Well, he still avoids the weddings. But we team up on most other jobs." She gave her friends a quick recap of a series of outdoor grad shoots they'd done. "And, Brenda, do you remember when I suggested doing engagement photos? They've been very well received, too."

"It does sound like you're booked up," Gracie said.

"I don't mind at all. My piggy bank loves it. The other night when Wyatt phoned, he said he'd stayed late to send Greg a tally of our sales for the month. Well, he couldn't believe how much we'd cleared."

Brenda held up her hand. "Hang on. Wyatt called you at home in the evening? That's very promising."

"He just wanted to check that I got home okay, Brenda. He knows my car's not too reliable. When I left it was so foggy I could hardly see the lines on the road. What's the matter?" Casey asked, noticing the three women gaping at her.

Brenda removed the pickles from her club sandwich the minute it came. "Nothing. I'd just told the girls I hardly hear from you anymore. So, has Wyatt replaced me as your new best friend?"

Casey set down her water glass and ate a piece of fruit that accompanied her chicken salad. "Of course not." But even as she spoke, she had to admit that her feelings for Wyatt had changed. Look how many times she'd lectured herself on the drive from Austin to Round Rock—warning herself not to fall in love with her boss. It was a prescription for heartache.

Gracie, ever the appeaser, reached across the table and squeezed Casey's arm. "Brenda's teasing. I'm happy Wyatt's getting back to his old self a bit more. Tom and I were talking about this the other day. Wyatt's far too young to give up on life."

Jana swallowed a bite of her sandwich. "I agree with Gracie. But, Casey, if you think Wyatt's beginning to look at you romantically, you need to—"

"He's not," she interrupted with such vehemence people at the next table glanced over at her.

"I think Jana was going to say you need to tell Wyatt you're pregnant," Brenda said, more solemnly than usual. "And she's right."

"Oh, really. Who has repeatedly told me not to say anything until he figures it out?" Brenda, of all people, knew how much Casey dreaded having that talk with Wyatt. But none of them knew how often he invaded her dreams. She imagined confessing almost every night. Sometimes, in her fantasies, he took the news in stride. But other times he was furious with her for lying, and threw her out of the studio.

"Don't be mad at Brenda," Gracie said. "We were all involved in keeping your secret."

"I'm not. I'm mad at me. When I told Wyatt the truth about Dane leaving me, I almost told him everything. I should have."

"And I talked you out of it," Brenda admitted.

"I'm not sorry you did. These extra months have been a godsend. I've pre-paid the hospital for the delivery. And I've saved enough for about a month after I have the baby."

"So why ruin a good thing?" Gracie's dark blue eyes flashed. "You say you feel fine. And you still don't look the least bit pregnant. I, for one, think the more time Wyatt has to get back to normal, the better. If he finds out that Casey's been deliberately keeping this from him, he won't just grieve for his baby again. He'll also feel really betrayed."

Brenda and Jana exchanged an unsure look.

Casey stabbed her salad with her fork. "That's exactly why I need to tell him sooner rather than later. Waiting just makes the betrayal worse. But I have to find the right time."

Brenda nodded vigorously. "We all know how much Wyatt wanted a baby. If Angela hadn't died…"

"She wouldn't have tried again," Jana countered. "If that's what you're hinting at. In fact, you're the one who said that even if Angela hadn't died, they might not have been able to conceive again after the ectopic pregnancy."

Brenda folded her napkin in her lap. "There are other methods. Artificial insemination, or using a surrogate."

"Knowing Angela, do you honestly think she'd have agreed to either of those?" Gracie asked.

The others didn't respond. It was Brenda who broke the silence. "I think I see what you're getting at, Gracie. It's no secret Wyatt wanted kids way more than Angela did. And she would never have slowed down enough to be a really involved mother. Her career meant too much."

Gracie reached for her purse to pay her check. "Maybe Wyatt will take an interest in Casey's baby."

"No, he won't." Casey didn't want her friends' fantasies to get out of hand. "I'm not sure he's made as much progress as you think. He avoids helping me with the weddings. It's as if he blames that wedding he shot in Angela's place for taking him out of town. I think he believes that if he'd been here, he could have saved her and their child."

Jana, usually the naysayer, nodded. "He still has a long way to go. But there's no refuting that Wyatt's improved since he hired you. I say keep the pregnancy to yourself awhile longer."

"Exactly," Gracie said, beaming. "Your baby's not due until February, right?"

"I know you mean well, but…" Casey searched for the right words. "But it's my decision."

Brenda passed the checks and payment to the harried waitress. "Don't rock the boat until after the holidays," she said. "This time of year's always rough for people who are grieving. There's no point adding to it if you don't have to."

"Plus, you'll save more money," Gracie added pragmatically. "If, heaven forbid, there are complications with the delivery, you'd be able to cover the higher costs."

Casey refused to be swayed. "Nothing's going to go wrong," she said adamantly. "The clinic doctor says I'm healthy as a horse."

"Casey's right. It's her choice," Brenda stated. "Honey, just consider waiting until after Christmas. Don't let the guilt and worry ruin the season for either of you. Our group set a date for our usual holiday dinner party and we'd love you to come. I want to see you wear that green silk dress with the black satin coat we made over."

"Me, too." Gracie clapped her hands excitedly.

"Wyatt may even join us," Jana added. "You could have knocked me over with a feather, Brenda, when you said Ian asked him and wasn't turned down flat."

"Oh, then I definitely can't come," Casey said. "I feel as if you're always shoving us together. I know Wyatt's noticed it, too. Brenda. You admitted you suckered him into checking on me the night of the team barbecue."

"Ian talked to him about the Christmas party, not me," Brenda said, standing up and putting on her jacket. "If you feel that strongly, Casey, I'll ask Greg to find out for sure if Wyatt plans to be there."

"Please," she said, falling into step with Brenda as the women left the café. "Thank you for coming to lunch. I have a bit of money. And I told myself I deserve a fun lunch out."

"You deserve more than that," Brenda said fiercely. "If I ever get a chance to meet Dane Sinclair, I'll smack him upside the head. You should hire a lawyer and go after him for child support."

"If she did that," Jana said, "he might try to get custody to avoid paying."

Casey sighed. "Dane would never want custody. He's made it perfectly clear he has no interest in being a father. And anyway, he's far too self-centered." She looked at her watch. "I need to get back to the studio in case Wyatt calls. He's out of town, and I didn't tell him about meeting you three."

"Why not?" Gracie asked.

"Well, you were Angela's friends first. I'd hate it if he thought I was trying to take her place personally as well as professionally."

Jana pursed her lips. "I'm not sure men think that way. Bless their hearts, they tend not to examine these things too deeply."

The women all laughed.

Since Gracie and Jana had driven together, they said goodbye at Jana's car. Brenda had parked farther away, as had Casey, so the two of them walked on together.

"Brenda, I have a big favor to ask you. I know you've been swamped lately. First the triplets were sick, then you were busy sewing Halloween costumes. I need a birthing coach. It's a lot to ask—it involves quite a few nights out, and whatever time I'm in labor."

"I'd love to, Casey, but I'll need to think about it. It's true life's been crazy at my house. Do you need an answer today? Do you have someone in mind if I can't?"

"I can ask Dolly Howell, my foster mother. I haven't told her and Len about the baby yet, but I need to soon. I want my baby to have grandparents. I've dragged my feet because my emotions are up and down. The past few weeks I've spent too much time comparing myself to my mom. Anyway, if I need her, I'm sure Dolly will come down from Dallas."

"What about your ex-mother-in-law? She's a grandmother, too."

"Yes, well. Mr. and Mrs. Sinclair don't know, either. I suppose I'll have to tell them soon if Dane doesn't."

"Say no more. The fact that you call them Mr. and Mrs. Sinclair speaks volumes."

"They're stuffy, but not horrible people. I just think it's Dane's place to tell them about his…our baby." Casey waved her hand, feeling too emotional.

Brenda hugged her. "I said it before and I'll say it again. You deserve more, Casey. And your baby will be better off without such cold relatives."

"I'd probably second that, but I know how hard it is to grow up without any extended family. I used to dream that my children would have aunts, uncles and grandparents. Most of all I wanted them to have a father. Why couldn't I see through Dane?"

Brenda shrugged as she watched Casey dry her eyes.

"You were blinded by love. That happens. Next time, you'll pick a better man."

The women said goodbye then. Casey started her car, her mind still on Brenda's words. Casey *had* picked a better man. Wyatt Keene. For all the good it did her. Wyatt had been so damaged by losing Angela, Casey doubted he'd ever love another woman.

THE MAN IN QUESTION was packaging orders when Casey entered the studio. He was wearing dark, snug jeans and a black T-shirt that complemented the coal color of his hair. A stray lock fell over his right eye. Glancing up at the sound of her footsteps, he pushed it back, only to have it fall again.

"Where have you been?" he demanded. "I checked the schedule but there's no off-site appointment listed. Nothing until the Hammond family comes in at two."

Casey took off her wool shawl and set it on the file cabinet with her purse. "I met Brenda for lunch. I thought you went to Rockdale to take pictures of puppies. I wasn't expecting you to be here or I would've let you know."

"Maybelle Dent canceled. She lives on a dirt road, and with the recent rains, it's been washed out. I wish you'd called me. If I'd known you were seeing Brenda, I'd have suggested Greg and I meet up with you for lunch."

Casey couldn't believe her ears. She and Wyatt had eaten together in the studio. But a meal out with friends? Was that too close to a date? She caught her breath just thinking about it. Even though that probably wasn't at all what he meant. As he continued to sit and stare at her, she mumbled, "Um, that would've been nice. Maybe next time."

"Casey, there's something I've been wanting to talk to you about." Wyatt sealed the last envelope and tossed it in a basket to be mailed with the others. He obviously didn't realize his hesitation and suddenly cool expression had caused Casey's heart to gallop in fear.

Had he noticed her baby bump? Did he now know she'd been lying to him the whole time? Her nervousness grew as he began to pace, all the while massaging the back of his neck. Finally he sighed heavily. "You know the wedding you have scheduled for Friday afternoon and evening?"

"Adison? Julie Adison and Luke DeVoe," Casey said, scrambling to remember the names.

"That's the one. I went to high school with Julie's brother, Tyler. Their dad used to be mayor of Uvalde. Now he's moved up and is a state representative here in Austin. According to Tyler, this wedding's going to be a huge frigging deal. I didn't know anything about it until he called me, asking me to personally oversee the shoot. It was more like a demand," Wyatt added as an afterthought.

"Wow. I knew it was a big affair, but I had no idea there were political associations, too. I met Julie and Luke at the golf resort where they're having the reception. It's totally ritzy. They're expecting five hundred guests. Julie's mom quadrupled our largest wedding package. Luke's mom wants the same amount." When Casey stopped to breathe, she felt the tension radiating from Wyatt. Then she realized the implication of what he'd said. "Wyatt, it won't hurt my feelings if you'd rather handle this alone. I can give you the orders I wrote up."

"That's the last thing I want," he snapped. "I've never liked waiting around through the ritual of weddings. And there's something about being *ordered* to be there that pisses me off. Beyond that…I haven't been near a wedding since…" He visibly clenched his jaw. "It's the first wedding since…" He tried again, but still couldn't finish the thought.

"It's okay, Wyatt. I know what you're trying to say."

He folded his arms across his chest and avoided her gaze.

Casey chewed her lip as she considered the next step. "You could tell them to find another photographer, except…it's terribly late. And we've got a contract. If we tried to get out of it now, it would be awful for the studio's reputation. All the hard work we've put in recently would be wasted. When I agreed to work them in, they were desperate because their first photographer had canceled. I had no idea you and they had a history. I thought doing a big event like this would be good for the studio."

"It is. You did nothing wrong. This thing I have about weddings is my problem, not yours." He waved a hand in the air, as though acknowledging his lack of progress.

"What you need is a haircut," Casey said, tilting her

head to one side. "And you'll need to wear a suit on Friday. I'll take the pictures. You can hang out with the bigwigs and make a good impression on the other guests."

Wyatt snorted. Then his lips twitched, and a faint smile lit his face. "I get the message, Casey. I need to give the clients what they want. I should attend, try not to mess up one of the biggest orders in the history of this studio, and leave you to do what you do best."

"*The* biggest order. I checked," she said smugly.

"Really? Angela would have loved this job," he said slowly, his smile fading. "All that society stuff meant more to her than to me. She put together an album of all her wedding photos that hit the society pages. She took it along whenever she met with a potential client."

"That's great advertisement. If somebody with a big name hires us, then we must be the best around. The bad part is you often have to take a lot of crap from people with that kind of stature."

"Don't I know it. That's why I resent Tyler calling me and underscoring his daddy's standing in Austin politics. Ty and I grew up playing ball together, sharing tuna sandwiches for lunch because that was all our families could afford back then." Wyatt shot Casey a hard look.

"I liked Julie and Luke. Her mom put on a few airs, but I've dealt with worse. She knows what she wants, but she's willing to pay for it. Some rich people expect tons of perks just because of who they are."

"Okay. I'll calm down. Ty could've asked for a

discount for old times' sake. He didn't. I'm probably just grumpy because it's a wedding."

"I love weddings," Casey said. "All brides are beautiful—like in a fairy tale. Unfortunately, not all grooms turn out to be the handsome prince," she said with a grimace.

"Did you have a fancy wedding?"

She forced a smile. "Me? I got married in blue jeans. Dane wore cargo shorts and Birkenstocks. He got a justice of the peace to come to the brewpub while we were in the middle of inventory. Two vendors we'd met just that day were our witnesses. I must have been out of my mind. A sane woman would've seen through that."

"Hmm." Wyatt picked up his car keys from the counter and put on a ball cap that hid his eyes. "I'll go get that haircut. And I'll drop these packets off with Mandy Axtell on my way. What else did you say I needed? Oh, yeah…a suit. I don't have one anymore. Maybe I'll wear leather and chains instead. Shake the place up. What do you think?"

If he was trying to get a rise out of Casey, he failed miserably. She just shrugged. "It's your company's reputation on the line, mister."

AFTER DROPPING OFF THE Axtell engagement pictures, Wyatt headed over to the barber's and felt his spirits lifting in spite of the chilly wind. A few months ago he couldn't have imagined working a wedding. But it might not be so bad with Casey. She was practical.

Wyatt liked that. She had a dry wit. And she wasn't easily thrown. He hadn't really thought about it before, but Casey was easy to spend long hours around. She was self-sufficient, but she didn't object when he offered help.

He'd liked Angela's self-sufficiency, as well. Until it killed her.

Was it terrible of him to admit that he sort of enjoyed feeling needed?

Whenever Wyatt let himself think back, he couldn't help but wonder what would have happened if Angela had allowed him to take her to the hospital that morning. Even as late as the lunch with her friends, anyone but Angela would've let a friend drive them to the doctor.

He supposed that, in some ways, his marriage and Casey's had been similar. They'd both gone into it hoping they'd found that perfect partner, someone who would share all of life's ups and downs. It was only later that they'd discovered that the ones they loved had never really needed them in return.

All through his time at the barbershop, Wyatt wondered if he might be making another mistake in letting competent, feisty and oddly vulnerable Casey Sinclair get under his skin.

Did she have the faintest idea how often she was in his thoughts? At night when he was trying to sleep, and at other inappropriate times. He shouldn't let himself dwell on how her idiot husband could take off and leave her life in such upheaval.

But he didn't know how to stop.

As he reached the mall, Wyatt realized that he was thinking about Casey more and more these days. And thinking about Angela less. Perhaps he was finally moving on.

In the men's clothing store, he chose a dark green wool suit and a gold tie for no reason other than he thought Casey would like them. Wyatt knew he'd turned a corner—and that his life would never be the same after today. He was even more convinced during the rest of the week when he found himself counting the days until the Adison-DeVoe wedding, not with dread but with anticipation.

FRIDAY DAWNED, BRINGING WITH it a frigid northeasterly wind. Morning newscasters predicted extreme shifts in the already cool weather. The rain-slicked streets were expected to turn icy by the evening rush hour.

Casey didn't know what to believe. During the two years she'd lived in Round Rock, she'd experienced downpours, fog and the threat of tornadoes. Sure, last winter there had been a few frosty mornings, but the frost had always melted by noon. After changing her mind about what to wear to work that would keep her warm, but still be dressy enough for a high-society wedding, she gave up and called Wyatt's cell phone.

"Have you seen the news?" she asked when he answered. "The weather forecast, I mean. If things get as bad as they say, do you think Julie Adison will need to rethink the photos she wanted taken by the lake?"

"I'm just in a coffee shop on my way to the studio. The prospect of an ice storm is all everyone's talking about. One old rancher said today reminds him of the winter he milked his cows and got icicles."

"Funny, but not helpful. I have an off-site family holiday shoot on my way in this morning. Can you call Julie Adison?"

"I have Tyler Adison's number right here. I'll ask him what the plan is and call you right back."

Wyatt clicked off, leaving Casey holding a dead phone. She stared into her closet some more while she waited for his call, wishing she had the right shoes to wear with the blue wool tunic and tapered black pants. Her strappy black heels looked best, but if she had to maneuver an icy parking lot, her smartest alternative would be black ballet slippers.

Wyatt called back. "The Adisons have been in a dither all morning. At this point, moving the photos inside the club is the least of their worries. The wedding's on for eight, so I said we'd be there at six to take the pre-ceremony pictures."

"Okay. Maybe the storm will have blown over by then."

"We can hope. Drive carefully, Casey."

"I'll be fine. Thanks to you I have good tires now. I'll see you around noon. Would you like me to pick up Chinese takeout for lunch?"

"That would be great."

After they hung up, Casey wrapped the heavy black shawl Brenda had provided to go with her more dressy outfits around her shoulders. She shivered in the wind, but all in all didn't think it was so terribly cold. Maybe the reports of the coming storm were exaggerated.

The Crane family had three children, including a two-week-old baby. "Your kids are adorable," Casey said to Abby Crane as she snapped photos of them in their holiday finery. "Baby Caitlyn is just beautiful."

"She was a month premature. She wasn't due until two weeks before Christmas."

"A month early?" Casey could barely process the idea. "Is that rare?" She had never seriously considered the possibility that her own baby could be premature. Now she worried that she might not have as much time to prepare as she'd expected.

"All three of my babies arrived early," Abby said. "Luckily, they've all been healthy. Caitlyn spent an extra six days in the hospital after I came home." She smiled down at the sleeping infant, and Casey reached for her camera. From then on, she captured images the parents would be proud to tuck into their holiday cards.

Once she'd climbed back in her car, she jotted a note to ask her doctor about the chances of delivering early. Casey couldn't get past the four weeks early Mrs. Crane had mentioned. If there was any possibility of that happening to her, it would be mid-January. Only two months away, and she had nothing ready. Beyond that, a preemie would probably need more medical care than she'd counted on. How would she afford the extra bills?

She switched mental gears, returning to the weather. Wind gusts buffeted her car along the highway. When she stopped at the Chinese restaurant it still was raining lightly, and not bitterly cold, just blustery. Even so, it was nearly one o'clock before she reached the studio.

Wyatt jumped up from the computer and grabbed the papers that flew about as Casey opened the back door. "That wind's a doozy."

"It feels even stronger than when I left home. Have you heard an updated forecast?"

Wyatt took the bags of food, set them down beside his desk and helped Casey remove her bulky shawl. "The radio's saying the wind's getting more erratic. Oh, good, you thought to grab plates and utensils."

They hunkered down to eat while the food was still relatively warm. "I'm going to upload the Crane pictures I took today," Casey said when she'd finished. "They have three of the cutest kids you could ever hope to see. The baby's positively gorgeous."

"You're always exclaiming over the kids you photograph. Do you ever wish you'd had some with whats-izname?"

"Dane," she blurted, panicking at the question. The phone rang, saving her from answering. She jumped to answer it, then took her time discussing their special New Year's packages with the caller.

The rest of the afternoon, Wyatt kept the radio tuned to the news station to get the latest weather reports. Thankfully, he didn't mention children again. Casey kept their conversation general, sticking mainly to general photography, and in particular the Adison wedding.

At five-fifteen Wyatt packed their camera bags. "Still only rain," he announced after a trip out to his car. He shook raindrops off his new, shorter haircut. "Do you want to ride with me? I have four-wheel drive if the weather gets ugly."

"But then you'd have to bring me back here, and that's out of the way for both of us. I'll drive myself. I may leave early if the storm looks really bad. The family will be happier having you wind things down."

Wyatt only rolled his eyes.

Shortly before they pulled up next to each other at the church, the rain changed to sleet. "You go on in out of this," Wyatt called. "I'll bring our gear. Take my umbrella. No sense both of us getting wet."

The church filled up fast. Two of the bridesmaids got held up in traffic and were late, making everyone antsy.

Casey took pictures of the bride and her other attendants getting dressed. She was relieved to see the stragglers blow in, complaining about the worsening weather. Julie glowed like all brides. Luke was a mess of nerves, but for the most part the couple held up well during the prewedding photos.

"I set up the video camera in the church balcony like you asked," Wyatt murmured, pulling Casey aside as the bridal party prepared to walk down the aisle.

"If you keep an eye on the video, I'll grab the flashless camera and sneak up behind the pulpit to get better pictures of the couple when they say their vows," she answered.

Wyatt didn't mention the weather, but it was on his

mind. He'd glanced out front a few times and thought the sidewalk appeared slicker. Not that there was anything he could do about that now.

Julie Adison's dad, the statesman, rose at the end of the ceremony and advised people not to linger at the church. "We want everyone to enjoy the meal and dancing at the club. Drive carefully, please. We also want everyone to get home safely."

IT WAS GOOD ADVICE, Casey thought as she pulled into the golf club parking lot. Sleet blew in circles. She ducked her head and hurried to the shelter of the lobby. "Look," she said, grabbing Wyatt's sleeve when he joined her. "Your jacket and my shawl are stiff with ice just from the short walk in. How do you feel about doubling up so we can shoot the required photos faster? Let them party all night if they'd like."

"I'm good with that. I want you to get home out of this mess before they close the highway. There's apparently black ice. I don't like the thought of you driving on that in the dark."

Casey was touched by his concern. "I'll be careful," she promised.

The two of them set about working in tandem, the way they had at the Granvilles' anniversary party. Casey stopped worrying that she'd pushed Wyatt into something that would make him unhappy. He seemed to be doing fine.

"Done," she said at last, once they'd checked off everything on her list.

"Let's go. I already made our excuses to Julie and Luke. I promised her parents proofs by Monday afternoon, so they're satisfied, too."

Wyatt helped Casey with her heavy shawl, then shrugged into his coat. He carried all of their equipment; Casey had the umbrella and one small bag. Once out of the front door, she slipped and almost fell down the steps to the parking lot. Wyatt quickly dropped his load and grabbed her arm, sliding a hand half around her waist to steady her. "Careful," he said, sounding breathless. "Are you okay?"

All Casey could do was worry about whether or not he'd noticed her thickening waist.

"I'm fine," she said. "Thanks. I'll see you Monday."

Taking care where she stepped, she made a beeline for her car. They'd parked next to each other. She got in to warm up her vehicle, leaving Wyatt to load their gear into his SUV. But when she turned her key, nothing happened. She tried again. There was a rattle and a series of clicks, but her car didn't start.

"You think it's a bad battery?" Wyatt poked his head through her open door. "Slide out a minute. Let me try."

Casey didn't see what he could do differently, but she got out and huddled next to the car.

He tried several times. "I'm afraid it's definitely your battery," he said, passing back her keys. He paused for a second, staring at the sleet gathering on her eyelashes. Then he climbed out of her car. "Lock it up. This isn't the night to try and find anyone to fix it. You can spend the night in my guest room."

"I sh-shouldn't," she stuttered through frozen lips. "Oh, all right." She capitulated when he glared at her. "Darned car. I have an appointment next week for Roy Mitchell to do a modified overhaul. I shouldn't have put it off."

"Good. I worry about you driving that thing around. It's not safe."

Casey settled into the passenger seat and warmed her hands over the heater. Beyond that, they spoke little on the drive across town. When Wyatt turned onto his street, he found his way blocked by a large branch that had broken off a tree. Other limbs littered the frosty blacktop. Swearing, he pulled over to the curb. He slid out, went around and helped Casey climbed down. Linking arms, they walked as fast as they could along the dark, treacherous road, arriving in his foyer drenched and out of breath.

"Your room is the first on the right," he said. "Go see how wet you are while I start a fire in the living room fireplace. We may well lose power soon."

"Do you, uh, have a robe?" Casey's teeth chattered. But as she watched him pass the room he'd said was hers and enter another, she hoped he wouldn't give her anything of Angela's. The first thing she'd seen as he snapped on the living room lamp was a photo on the mantel of a woman who must be his wife. The late Mrs. Keene had olive skin and raven hair, and looked almost as tall as Wyatt. Casey was relieved to see that she really wasn't his type. So even if she was attracted to him, he'd never be interested in her.

"I don't own a robe," Wyatt said, coming back and handing Casey a thick flannel shirt instead. "It's clean and dry. Don't scowl. It's the best I can do. And it'll hang past your knees so don't be shy. Damn, there goes our power," he muttered as they were suddenly plunged into darkness. "Give me your hand. Here's a flashlight I grabbed while I was in my bedroom. I think there's wood laid in the fireplace. After you change, come out and get warm by the fire." He snapped on the flashlight, and all Casey could think was how ghoulish they both must look in the sickly yellow light. She tried to ignore that inner voice screaming that the jig was up.

But it was no use. Supposing she could even button Wyatt's flannel shirt around her expanding waist, there's no way she could hide the bulge of a baby who had already begun to kick.

It was all too much. Tonight's disaster was the final straw. Clutching the shirt and the wobbly flashlight, Casey slid down the wall to the cold wood floor. Feeling damp and chilled, she laid her head on her knees and began to cry.

CHAPTER NINE

"WHAT IS IT, CASEY?" Wyatt dropped to his knees beside her and gently stroked her back as she sobbed. "Are you hurt?"

"No. No. No." She shook her head, apparently unable to say more.

"Then what's the problem? I can't help if I don't know what's wrong."

She hugged his flannel shirt to her breast. "If I wear this, Wyatt, you'll see what I've been keeping from you from day one."

"What are you talking about?"

"I'm pregnant, Wyatt. My baby's due in February."

The house was so still, Casey's tearful confession might as well have been screamed. Wyatt jerked his hand away and bounded to his feet. The beam from his flashlight bobbed wildly across the cream-colored wall. His first reaction was disbelief. Followed by a sense of betrayal and jealousy mixed with…anger. Yes, anger. He'd become possessive of her. He shouldn't have, but it'd happened.

Casey angled her own flashlight better to see Wyatt's

face. She wanted to explain. "I knew things were wrong in my marriage. When I found out I was having a baby, I thought the news would make Dane happy, would settle him down. Instead, he said awful things and left. He'd already made plans to sell the pub and leave me."

When Casey paused for breath, she realized she was wasting her time. Wyatt's disbelief changed to the anger she'd had nightmares about. He thought he'd been deceived. And why not? She should have told him the whole truth from the beginning. She knew it. Had always known. Deep down, she'd known how it would all end. Just as she'd known she couldn't let her heart be shredded again.

Struggling to her feet, she knocked into a still-stunned Wyatt as she bent to grab her dripping shawl. Flinging it around her head and shoulders, she gathered what remained of her pride. "Don't worry about how you're going to fire me, Wyatt. I quit. Greg can send my last check to my home address. You can keep my camera until you upload tonight's wedding photos." Wrenching open the front door, she fled into the sleet-slicked night.

Wind whipped down the hall until the door closed behind her. Wyatt had difficulty making sense of what had just happened. He hadn't processed a word after Casey dropped the bombshell that she was pregnant. He berated himself for missing the signs that now seemed obvious. The ginger tea. The shapeless clothing. More to the point—why hadn't she told him months ago? But he knew. He wouldn't have given her the job. My God, he'd sent her running all over town. There were risks associated with pregnancy. He knew that better than anyone. And he'd condoned her driving that wreck of a car back and forth in all kinds of weather.

His gut twisted at the thought of what could have happened. Almost simultaneously, he realized how much his personal feelings for Casey had grown over the past few months. He looked forward to her arrival at the studio every morning. She had an infectious laugh that had brought joy back into his life. In the short time that he'd known her, she'd chased away the worst of his depression. He couldn't stay mad at her. Uncurling his fists, he said her name—to begin making amends. "Casey…"

He slowly shook himself out of his stupor. Casey wasn't there. She'd left in a huff. To go where? And how? Her car was still at the resort.

"Lord have mercy!" Patting his empty pockets for his keys, Wyatt thought about the ice storm and the broken branches blocking his street.

Casey was out there somewhere. With fear gripping his chest, he finally found the flashlight he'd dropped on the floor, and located the car keys he'd tossed on the credenza in his entryway. Not bothering to stop for his jacket, Wyatt raced out of the house. *What the hell had Casey meant, saying she quit?* He forced himself to concentrate on keeping his balance on the icy asphalt.

Wyatt fully expected to meet Casey coming back. With no transportation and only a shawl to protect her from the weather, surely she'd understand that her only option was to return to his house.

But his street was abandoned. Wyatt flashed his light into the line of trees on either side in case she'd taken shelter from the howling wind.

There was no sign of her.

Ice crystals stung Wyatt's face. In minutes, he was wet to the skin. Casey's shawl had been soggy to start with; her flimsy shoes were only for show. Wyatt didn't like thinking about how cold and wet she'd be by now.

He hurried down the block to the first intersection. Stopping, he wheeled one way, then another. His heart banged like drums in his ears as his breath escaped in frozen white puffs. Wyatt had no idea which street Casey had taken. And when had he seen a blacker night? No streetlights, no moon. Not a soul in sight.

Slipping, sliding, half falling, he made his way back to his SUV, gunned the engine and backed up the street, his wheels spinning. Turning around, he found a clear route back to the intersection.

Once there, he sat and drummed his thumbs on the steering wheel. He'd recently read an article in a magazine that said people tended to automatically turn in the direction of their dominant hand. He would've turned right, but Casey was left-handed. Wyatt had watched her work around the studio—had watched her a lot—and he'd grown used to placing her mug of tea on the left side of her computer.

Praying the article was correct, he turned left. At first, as his gaze followed the path illuminated by his headlights, Wyatt feared he'd guessed wrong. Then, he saw her. A small figure in the distance, struggling uphill against the wind. His relief was enormous until he saw her slip and go down hard on one knee.

Wyatt stepped on the gas, trying to speed to her rescue, and almost spun out. His damp hands had trouble holding on to the steering wheel.

Her fall, however, allowed him to catch up.

OVER THE STINGING, WHISTLING wind, Casey heard a car approaching. She turned to look, half hopeful, half afraid it might not be a Good Samaritan. Recognizing Wyatt's SUV, she whipped back around, but slipped and fell again.

Sensing him as he stopped next to her, she picked herself up and did her best to look dignified as she marched along the slippery sidewalk away from him. It was a pathetic attempt, and sapped her breath.

Rolling down his window, Wyatt discovered he didn't know what to say. He was afraid of screwing things up worse, so he got out of the car and scrambled after her. Catching her by the elbow, he brought her to a halt. "Casey, it's twenty degrees out here. I'll grant you I was shocked by what you told me. I acted like a jerk and I'm sorry. I...please come back to the house. We'll dry off, get warm and talk rationally."

"I *am* rational. I haven't been until now, but I suddenly am," she said, wiping a hand over her face. "It's freezing. I have no right to ask, Wyatt, but will you give me a lift to my car? I have Roy Mitchell's card in my glove box. Maybe I can talk him into coming to get me. It shouldn't take long for him to install a new battery so I can go home. I...I need to do that."

She was shivering so hard she was stuttering. Wyatt knew she hated to ask him for help. He saw what it cost her and was humbled. He released her elbow to grasp her hand and held on. By force of will he kept them both on their feet as he helped her downhill to where he'd left the SUV. Once they were settled inside and he'd turned up the heat, he pointed out the windshield. "Look around, Casey. The whole city's covered in ice. I don't want to seem like I'm bullying you, but it's too risky to drive to the resort. Riskier still for you to drive to Round Rock tonight, even if Roy agreed to fix your car, which I sincerely doubt."

Casey sat back in the passenger seat with a weary sigh. "You're right. It was dumb of me to run out. I'm not usually so irresponsible," she said, closing her eyes. "At least I wasn't before I started working for you."

Wyatt said nothing. He concentrated on conrolling the SUV on the slick, downhill stretch of road. Faced again with the blocked street, he got out and muscled the huge branch aside, clearing enough space to drive on the shoulder. A spot where he could maneuver around smaller broken branches. He navigated the stretch slowly and eventually made it home. Punching his garage door opener, he swore when it didn't work. He climbed down and opened the door by hand, then drove in out of sleet that had begun to freeze on his windshield.

After rounding the Subaru to open Casey's door, he said, "The power is likely to be out awhile, but I'm betting there's enough hot water left in the tank for you to warm up with a shower. I'll change my clothes after I start that fire I promised you."

The entrance from his garage led to the kitchen. Casey stopped just inside the door. "I feel awkward coming back here, Wyatt."

"Awkward or not, there's no sense in either of us catching pneumonia. There's a bath connected to the room I showed you. I, ah, believe the flannel shirt is still in the hall where you dropped it. I have sweats, but you'd swim in them." He handed her a flashlight. "Go on," he said gently. "I want to bring in extra wood for the fire."

Her shoes were wet, so she left them by the garage door and made her way barefoot down the hall.

Wyatt watched her until the flashlight's beam disappeared. He welcomed the darkness. A hundred unexpected emotions attacked him. The first was guilt at having a woman other than Angela spending the night in his home.

In the months after his wife's death, he had painted away her influence on every room. Angela had liked hanging pictures of herself everywhere. He had cleared out all of them except for one he'd left on the mantel. As for their baby, he hadn't kept a single reminder. He'd carted bags full of things to Goodwill, including the baby gifts Angela's friends had given her at lunch the day she died. After seeing the first one, a rattle,

Wyatt had left the others wrapped. The very thought of Casey being pregnant sent waves of fear shuddering through him.

Kicking himself into action, he went out to gather an armload of wood. He heard the shower running as he knelt to put a match to the dry kindling already set up in the fireplace. Once the first thin flame caught and the wood began to crackle, he stood and gazed at Angela's photograph. He found it hard to believe that thinking about her didn't hurt as much as it had a few months ago when Greg suggested reopening the studio. Nor did the house feel half as lonely tonight, he thought, as he went to his room and stripped off his wet clothing. For the past year he'd tried to understand why it had felt so lonely. Angela had spent most nights working late at the studio.

Even though he went to change several minutes after Casey's shower shut off, Wyatt emerged before she did. It had grown so quiet in the guest room he wondered if she'd fallen asleep. Or was she hiding in there, avoiding the talk he'd suggested?

He was back in the living room, putting another log on the fire, when he sensed her presence. Replacing the poker in its rack, he got to his feet, and saw Casey peering around the door frame. In the flickering fire-light, Wyatt saw that she was wearing his old flannel shirt. It barely buttoned over her rounded belly, but he pretended not to notice.

Casey gestured with a soggy bundle. "I left most of my clothes hanging in the bathroom to dry. If I may, I'll set my shoes by the fire. It's possible they'll survive, although the soles are in danger of disintegrating. If you'll point me in the direction of your laundry room, I'll throw my, uh, undies in the dryer for a few minutes."

"I'll do that. You come sit by the fire." Wyatt shook out an afghan lying on one end of the couch, as a means to entice her.

She wasn't swayed. "I'd ra-rather, uh… You don't need to take care of my personal things."

"I've done lots of laundry in my life, Casey, some of it even 'personal.' But suit yourself. The washer and dryer are behind bifold doors at the top of the stairs." He pointed the way, and Casey turned and skittered right up them. Wyatt couldn't resist admiring the flash of bare legs as she climbed, holding her flashlight. Shapeless as his old shirt was hanging on her small frame, the hem hit her midthigh and left a tempting length of pale leg exposed. As much as Wyatt liked how Casey looked, the sudden curl of heat below the belt told him he probably ought to focus on something else. That was when he realized he'd been so busy ogling Casey's cute backside, he'd forgotten the power was out.

He called up to her, "Wait. You can't use the dryer without electricity."

"Do I feel silly," she said, carefully picking her way back downstairs. "I found another hanger on your washer, though," she said, and Wyatt saw that she'd clipped her bra and panties to it. "Uh, I'll hang this with the rest of my things," she added lamely.

Wyatt still gripped the blanket. He crossed to where

she lingered on the first step and wrapped it around her shoulders. Taking the hanger, he hooked it on the bannister.

"They'll dry faster near the fire. Come. I pulled the rocker close to the hearth for you." He led her to the chair.

"You have a very nice home," she said, to make small talk as she tucked her feet under her and arranged the blanket over her bare legs.

"It's too big for me. I thought about selling." Wyatt sat on the end of the sofa nearest Casey's chair. He propped his forearms on his thighs and clasped his hands between his knees. "But the market went to hell."

"Compared to this, my house is a cracker box. I considered selling, too, but a Realtor told me the same thing—I'd never get my money back. Funny, my first argument with Dane was about buying it in the first place. He wanted to keep renting the apartment. But his folks gave us money as a wedding present that they specifically said was for a down payment. To me, owning a home spelled permanence. As it happens, Dane took out an equity line of credit, so even buying a home doesn't guarantee security." Casey stared into the dancing flames, and her voice trailed off slowly.

"You've got that right. With us, I was the one who argued to buy a house. All Angela wanted was to open a studio."

"You were always both photographers?"

"Yes. We met in college."

"Love at first sight, huh?"

Wyatt smiled crookedly, thinking back as the fire sizzled and snapped. "My first impression of Angela was that she'd come from privilege. Her take-charge attitude, I suppose. She led a project we were assigned. In reality, Angela grew up in a group home, and had a hardscrabble life. I was one of few people she ever let close enough to know that. The day we got married I promised I'd always be there for her—for the scared, not-so-confident person she was at her core. But…" Wyatt hung his head. "When push came to shove I wasn't around when she needed me most. For her or our baby."

"I'm so sorry you had to go through that," Casey said. Her heart suddenly felt squeezed tight. "You should never have had to deal with me lying to you, too. I just didn't know what else to do. My second day on the job I met Brenda. She guessed that I was pregnant and felt bad for me. After she explained why you'd closed the studio, I was terrified to say anything, to be honest. I thought about it, and came to the conclusion it'd be better if I waited awhile. Brenda offered me her old maternity clothes and she, Gracie and Jana altered them so you wouldn't see the truth. I shouldn't have done that, but I did. Please don't blame your friends. They were just glad to see you get back to work. All I can do is apologize again, Wyatt. I truly hated lying to you."

"Did you think I'd be a total hard-ass, or what?"

"No. I thought you were a man of principle, who still hurt after losing your wife and child. The night of the

Granvilles' party, I wanted to confess everything. Then I saw how shocked and angry you were at finding out I'd let you think I was married when I was already divorced." Casey rubbed her temples in frustration as she completed her sentence.

"I still find it unforgivable that any man could leave his wife in such dire straits. Especially if he knew she was carrying his baby."

"Dane didn't like being tied down."

"What did he expect you to do?"

She shrugged, and idly picked at the fringe on the blanket. "He didn't say. He barely even said goodbye. I learned the day after he took off that he'd sold the microbrewery without telling me, too." She ruffled her drying hair. "My ex-husband is a poster child for the me-first generation. If he gave any thought to me at all, he probably assumed I'd go back to Dallas—where we met when I photographed his sister's wedding. I suppose it's my fault for insisting on marriage when he wanted me to move down here and just live with him. Can we not talk about Dane anymore?" she said with a toss of her curls.

"As long as I can reiterate that I think he's slime, sure, let's change the subject. Tell me about your child-hood. You've mentioned your foster parents more than once. I gather you weren't always in the foster care system."

Casey shifted in the rocker. "No. Until I was thirteen it was just me and my mom. She had a bad heart and couldn't work. We lived on welfare, but her medicine alone was so expensive we rarely had enough to buy food. I will provide better for my baby," she said fiercely, her voice brittle. "I have to."

Wyatt doubted she was aware that the blanket had slipped below her waist. Or that she had begun to rub both hands over the slight mound that now was quite visible under her shirt. He was more affected than he imagined he'd be by her gutsy determination to have and raise a baby by herself.

"I wanted a big family," he murmured, leaving the couch and kneeling at her side. It seemed natural to curl his large hand over her smaller, restless one. "At least four boys and girls. It's why we bought a five-bedroom house with a huge backyard, even though it was just the two of us."

Casey stopped moving her hand. "I keep thinking of the baby as a girl, but I really don't care which I have. I'll be happy with either." Her mouth suddenly rounded in surprise. "I just felt a kick."

Wyatt jerked away, then stared at where his hand had been.

"Would…you like to feel?" she asked hesitantly.

His eyes darkened, but he let her guide his fingers to her stomach. "There, I felt it," he said. He gazed up at her in awe. "Uh, when does the kicking start? Angela wasn't that far into her pregnancy. But you hardly… show." Wyatt's ears turned red.

"I know. The nurses at the clinic joke that the kid's hanging on to my backbone. Brenda, Gracie and Jana say it's remarkable that I don't look like I swallowed a basketball, given how short I am. Apparently they all did. But how lucky is it not to have a waistline anymore? I'm beginning to feel like a blimp."

"You fooled me," he said, their eyes locking.

Casey touched his face. "I'm sorry. I'll say it as many times as you'd like."

"No. I didn't mean fool me as in misled me. I mean, I thought you were stylish, and…well, I liked what I saw. No one would ever take you for a blimp." Wyatt ran his hands up and down her arms. "I hate when you look sad, like now. I've noticed it at the studio sometimes. I want to make things better. What can I do?"

"Nothing. Maybe this weather has made me depressed. Or the car. What if it can't be fixed, Wyatt? I'll feel…cut adrift. Especially since I quit working for you."

"Quit? You did say that, but…" Springing up, Wyatt drew Casey to the sofa with him and settled her on his lap. "We need to talk about your schedule. You can't dash all over the city, taking home appointments, or go running off to evening weddings. I'll take on more," he said earnestly. "Or else I'll drive you to events and we'll team up—like tonight. Until that gets to be too much."

"Wyatt, are you saying you still want me to work for you? I quit because I couldn't bear to have you fire me, even if I deserved it."

"You're not fired, and I won't let you quit. I need you, Casey." His voice shook with fervency and something more.

Overcome by joy, Casey forgot to be cautious. She pressed a hand to each side of his face and planted a kiss right on his lips. She'd meant it to be the kind of kiss they'd look back on and maybe laugh about. She hadn't reckoned on Wyatt threading his fingers into her hair and increasing the urgency until the air around them sparkled.

After being lonely for so long, Casey fell right under his spell Caught up in the moment, she trailed her fingers over Wyatt's cheeks, then down his neck, until finally she flattened her hands on his chest, where she reveled in the strong beating of his heart. Even if she'd tried, she probably couldn't have controlled the little sounds of pleasure that left her lips.

WYATT'S MIND WENT BLANK the minute Casey's soft lips touched his. He'd watched those lips at the office as she talked animatedly on the phone to clients. Had watched her enjoy a sandwich. Seen her unconsciously nibble on the end of her pen when she concentrated.

He would shift uncomfortably, or get up and leave the studio. During those times, he hadn't dared imagine tasting her lips. Now he didn't have to imagine anymore. And she tasted way better than he'd ever thought.

She looked lush and delectable, too, in the golden glow from the fire. He wanted to see and taste more of her.

Casey made a weak attempt to cover her breasts as Wyatt nimbly unbuttoned her borrowed shirt. He gave a little shake of his head and stayed her hands. "You're beautiful," he murmured, silencing her garbled objections that she felt fat.

The heat in his eyes sucked Casey in. At that moment she felt…loved. She ignored any lingering concerns and gave herself over to Wyatt's tender attention.

He never directly mentioned her baby, but as he kissed her belly he asked if he should stop, or if it was safe for her to make love.

"It's fine," she said, shivering. She didn't want him to stop his exploration of her body. "I'm perfectly healthy, so there's no reason to worry. Please, Wyatt," she added, running her hands over his bare shoulders. She wasn't sure when he'd stripped off his sweatshirt but she loved the feel of his skin. "Please, don't stop."

He didn't, thank heaven.

Wyatt took such care, Casey felt as if this was her first time making love. She wasn't used to such a considerate, generous partner. Wyatt made sure she was satisfied before he sought relief.

Some time later, when they drifted down from the most passionate high, Wyatt pulled the blanket over them both. He tucked her to him and pressed his lips against the sweet spot just below her left ear. And in the half hour she spent in his arms before sleep claimed both of them, Casey treasured all his whispered endearments.

But, even so, she didn't kid herself that this could last any longer than the storm that raged outside. They'd simply shared some of the human warmth that had been missing from their lives. She silently wished it would never end, all the while knowing it would.

CASEY WOKE UP AND LANGUIDLY stretched her arms above her head. It was dark except for a faint glow of embers burning low in the fireplace. *Wait*—she didn't have a fireplace. For a second she struggled to remember where she was and why. Then the events from the night before crashed over, and she realized the weight across her middle was Wyatt's arm.

The two of them had changed places sometime in the night and she now lay on the edge of the sofa, with him pressed into the cushions.

Guilt flooded her. *Had she really just slept with her boss?* What on earth had she been thinking? How would she ever be able to face him at work? She'd abandoned her good sense for one night in Wyatt's arms and no doubt ruined their professional relationship.

Slipping out from under Wyatt's arm, she covered her nakedness with the flannel shirt, grabbed her undies and all but ran down the hall. The tunic and pants she'd hung in the bathroom were only slightly damp. The heavy wool shawl felt cold. She didn't care, she decided, yanking them on with shaking fingers.

Her shoes were stiff but dry. They would get her where she needed to go. Still, Casey couldn't help taking one last, loving glance at Wyatt, relaxed and rumpled in sleep.

What they'd done last night had been thoroughly unprofessional. Casey had listened to him speak of how he'd met Angela. And how guilty he felt about not being able to protect her. He glossed over her death, and the loss of their baby, but Casey had sensed his anguish. Somehow, she'd fallen in love with Wyatt. She thought she'd told him. He hadn't returned the sentiment.

Casey rubbed at an ache lodged near her heart. She needed to leave before Wyatt woke up. How awkward it would be to face each other.

Considering what a kind man he was, Wyatt probably would apologize and repeat that she still had the job. She'd rather leave and remember the night they'd shared as something special, even if she knew it meant more to her than it did to Wyatt.

Perhaps she could pull off acting unaffected. A modern woman to whom a one-night-stand was no big deal.

So why were there tears running down her cheeks as she slipped out Wyatt's front door?

A block from the house she phoned for a taxi. Last night's sleet had turned into a misty rain. While she paced on the corner, waiting for the cab to show up, Casey tried to tell herself it was only rain she was wiping from her face.

WYATT ROLLED OVER, EXPOSING his bare back to cold air. He awoke enough to realize how contented and relaxed he felt in spite of the chill in the room. Casey got all the credit for that. He couldn't remember the last time he'd greeted a day feeling this rested and…carefree—

a term that hadn't applied to him since at least a year before Angela died. Those months she'd been insanely busy. Wyatt couldn't remember a single time she'd made it to bed prior to his falling asleep.

Except the night she got pregnant.

All at once, he came fully awake and shot bolt upright. He was naked on his sofa, except for a blanket that barely covered his legs. The power was still out. The fire was stone cold. His sweats lay crumpled on the floor.

Casey. Wyatt kicked off the blanket, threw on his sweatpants and hustled down the hall to the guest room. The most likely scenario was that he'd taken up too much space on the couch and she'd gone to sleep in the bed.

She wasn't there, nor in the bathroom or kitchen. For a minute he stood in the middle of the living room and wondered if the previous night had been a dream. But he knew it was real.

Why had she left like that? Without waking him to say goodbye? Apparently the night they'd shared meant nothing to her. And that upset Wyatt.

It wasn't until he stepped beneath an icy shower that he started to worry that maybe he'd hurt her. What if he hadn't been careful enough last night? What if their lovemaking caused her to lose the baby? What if she'd been in trouble but couldn't wake him?

Shutting off the shower, he jumped into his jeans and a clean sweatshirt. He punched in Casey's cell number, but it went straight to voice mail. Then he called her at home as he struggled to keep the phone to his ear and pull socks on over still-damp feet. He got no answer. *She wouldn't answer if she was at the hospital, you fool.*

With his heart pounding like a kettledrum, Wyatt reran an all-too-familiar drive to a hospital he'd hoped never to set foot inside again.

"ARE YOU QUITE SURE no one admitted Casey Sinclair in the last few hours?" he demanded of a receptionist who was beginning to cast her eyes around for a security guard. He made a conscious effort to calm down. "I'm not a nutcase," he said. "Casey works for me. She's pregnant, about six or so months along. I can't reach her on her home phone. We worked late last night," he said inanely. "She had car trouble and given the magnitude of the storm... Are you positive she's not here? She lives in Round Rock." Wyatt stopped then, knowing he probably did sound unhinged.

The receptionist typed something into her computer. "I'm sorry, sir, I don't see her listed as even having been treated and released from Emergency. Could be she's merely stuck in traffic. Or maybe she decided to spend the night in a motel instead of going all the way home."

The woman's placid smile irritated Wyatt. He wanted to shout that he knew Casey hadn't gone home last night. She'd spent most of it with him, making wild, passionate love, and that was why he was so damn worried.

He didn't share that information with the matronly

clerk, although in her position she'd probably seen and heard it all.

"Is there a hospital in Round Rock?"

She handed him a telephone book from under the counter. "The numbers should all be in this."

Wyatt flipped through the book, found three medical centers in the Round Rock area. He copied their numbers on a page he ripped from a magazine, then ran out to his SUV and began calling.

It took time to work his way through the numbers to find out that no Casey Sinclair had been treated at any local hospital. Between calls, Wyatt again tried reaching her at home, to no avail. He knew he should be relieved to learn she hadn't been hospitalized, but instead his worry escalated. After all, Angela had suffered her trauma at the side of the road.

Wyatt was about to start the Subaru when his cell rang. He flipped it open, hoping to hear Casey's voice. His caller was Roy Mitchell.

"Hey, Wyatt, I've been trying to get hold of you half the morning."

"I've been searching for Casey," Wyatt said.

"That's who I'm calling about. She just left my shop. She called me at an unholy hour to come give her a tow. I replaced her battery, but that starter's not gonna last. She's got an electrical problem someplace. Wouldn't let me do any diagnostics because she can't afford to put any more money in that junker right now. Damn fool woman needs a new vehicle. She didn't want to hear that, either. She mentioned having to save money for when she has her baby. I didn't even know she was pregnant. All I know is someone oughta talk some sense into her. I thought if you have any influence as her boss…or maybe you don't. She strikes me as pretty independent. Anyway, I said I could get her a good deal on a safer used car. My offer stands in case you can convince her. I'm heading home now, but let me know either way. I was out all night towing cars that spun out during that storm. It was something, wasn't it?"

"A mess," he agreed, his mind racing. Profound relief swept over him, followed by fury. Didn't she know he'd be worried sick about her?

After Roy hung up, Wyatt sat a minute staring out the windshield. He'd convinced Casey to stay with him instead of phoning Roy, who Wyatt insisted wouldn't come out in a storm to tow her. If Roy told her he'd worked all night, she probably thought Wyatt had said that just to get her into bed. That couldn't be further from the truth. Well, maybe subconsciously… Because if a genie appeared and granted him three wishes, there wasn't a damn thing he'd change about last night.

He had to see Casey and work this out.

CHAPTER TEN

IT'D BEEN YEARS SINCE Wyatt had been to Round Rock. The town was bigger than he remembered. Casey's home, when he finally found it, sat across from a quiet neighborhood park. His first thought, after he stopped behind her beater car, was that this would be a pleasant place to raise children. Which Casey would do. She had a life here that didn't include him. As she should. She'd have friends and neighbors to watch out for her and the baby.

With the speed of light, Wyatt switched mental gears. He didn't want to think about Casey having a baby. He only needed to make sure she was okay after last night—that he hadn't hurt her.

He hated worrying, and hated feeling guilty even more. He'd had quite enough of both, thank you. He *did* feel guilty as hell for initiating what had happened between them last night. Wyatt wished he could blame his actions on alcohol or some other factor. Except he hadn't touched a drop. Try as he might to make their night together insignificant, he couldn't.

He knocked on her door, steeling himself for—well, anything.

CASEY HEARD A KNOCK at her door. She was in the middle of pulling on an oversize T-shirt over comfy sweats. She'd been home just long enough to get out of yesterday's clothes. Smoothing down the soft cotton, she padded barefoot to the door and rose on tiptoes to look through the peephole. The last person she expected to see was Wyatt. Yet there he stood, hands jammed in his pockets, rocking back and forth on his heels. Casey's breath caught in her throat. Her first inclination was to duck and ignore his knock.

He pounded harder, and she knew she had to answer. Composing herself, she smoothed a hand over her jumpy stomach and cracked the door open a few inches. Keeping hold of the knob, she dredged up a weak smile.

Wyatt's gaze slowly traveled from her bare toes and all the way up to her wary hazel eyes. "If you'd ever worn that to work, I would've guessed the truth immediately. And everything would've been different."

Casey tossed her head. "I knew that in the cold light of day you'd change your mind about accepting my resignation. I understand…really."

"May I come in?"

She still didn't open the door any wider. "That's not necessary. Greg can send anything you still owe me. I'll explain to Brenda that I couldn't continue the charade."

"We need to discuss—" Wyatt broke off when Casey shivered. "It's still cold as a well-digger's knees out here, and your feet are bare. Let's talk inside, where you'll be warmer."

"There's nothing to say I…we crossed a line last night."

"Are you okay? You're really pale."

Casey's hand flew to her face, letting go of the door. Wyatt barged right in and shut it behind him.

She stood her ground, but crossed her arms and rubbed at the goose bumps.

So as not to crowd her, he stepped away, taking in the neat, minimally furnished room.

"Since you're here, you may as well have a seat." She gestured to the sofa. "I can make you a cup of coffee. I'm afraid I've only got instant."

"No need to go to that trouble." Wyatt sat gingerly on her hard, narrow sofa. He was immediately reminded of how they'd made love on his larger, comfier one. He stood and moved to a straight-backed chair instead.

"Look," she said, running a hand through curls she hadn't taken time to comb. "If you're afraid I'll hold last night over your head, or expect our relationship to… change in some way, don't worry. I know what happened was a complete aberration."

"An aberration?" Wyatt frowned, not liking the word at all.

"I shouldn't have kissed you. That was a dumb thing to do. Irresponsible. I apologize."

Wyatt's jaw hardened. "I accept my share of the blame," he said stiffly. "I'll get straight to the reason I'm here. I regret that I could have hurt…ah…you. I'd never have forgiven myself." He got up and paced around the small room. Stopping at the window, he turned, his tense jaw twitching nervously. "Casey, you know I think your photos are superb. But if you stay on we'll need to adjust your schedule. And…it's essential we go back to being studio owner and employee."

Once the words were out, sounding too loud in the otherwise still room, Wyatt had trouble drawing that line in his mind. His gaze fell on Casey's mouth as she trapped her bottom lip between her teeth, then let it go and soothed the spot with her tongue.

Raising his shoulders and letting them drop, he exclaimed, "Why did you take off without waking me up?" It was the last thing he'd intended to ask.

"I didn't want you to act all formal and stiff like you are acting now. We can't take back what we did, Wyatt," she said, throwing up her hands. She couldn't tell him the truth. She didn't want things to change. But she'd instinctively known they would. "If that's all you wanted to know, you can go now. We'll both have until Monday to decide if we can work together." Casey moved toward the door. "I believe I'm mature enough to put last night aside for the sake of business. Are you?"

"What? Of course. However, before you throw me out, there's one other item that's bugging me. Your car—and I use the term loosely. According to Roy Mitchell it's a death trap."

"You talked to Roy?"

"He phoned me. It seems he gave you advice you brushed off. He thought that, as your employer, I might be able to help. You know, give you an advance or something."

"You already advanced me money for the tires."

"And you paid that back. Roy told you he could get you a great deal on a safer, used car?"

She shrugged. "He mentioned he'd overhauled a Toyota for a guy who buys and sells cars on a small scale."

"If Roy can find you something with air bags, that'd be a good start. I drove that highway today, Casey. With big trucks passing me every few minutes, and the pavement slick with rain. You can't keep driving that road in an unsafe car. It's too risky. Find some shoes and get your coat. Maybe he'll take your car in trade. Let's see what kind of deal we can wangle."

"Wyatt, I appreciate your coming all this way, and your concern. But I…can't take on extra debt. Even if I work up to my due date, my doctor suggests taking six weeks off after the birth. That's supposing I can find infant child care." Casey curled her hands into fists. "Thank you, but no. I can maybe swing having Roy tune up my Honda next month, but no more than that."

"What if I make it a condition of continuing to work with me?"

"I'd say that's sneaky," she retorted.

He shoved his fingertips in his back pockets and continued to stare her down.

Casey broke eye contact first. "I want to keep my job. The doctor says I'm fit as a fiddle. This isn't fair, Wyatt."

"Probably not. What if I make a deal with Roy? I'm sure Greg could write off the expense of a company car for you to drive. Would you agree to that? I can't bear worrying about you driving all over hell's half acre in that ancient Honda. Especially now that Roy's told me what kind of shape it's really in."

Feeling tears prickle her eyes, Casey had to turn away. It had been a long time since she'd felt so cared for. Her throat closed up again. "Saying thank-you doesn't seem enough."

"It's just good business sense. You've brought in the lion's share of my profits since you started. Let's go visit Roy." Wyatt refused to even consider that there might be more motivating his offer than merely business.

Casey capitulated because it was the sensible thing to do. They drove straight to Mitchell's Garage, speaking only when necessary.

At the garage, Roy explained that he knew a man who wanted to sell his Toyota, and gave Wyatt the price.

"That's reasonable," Wyatt said. "Will you take half down and carry a contract on the remainder?"

"I'll vouch for you." Roy made a call and within ten minutes a man drove up in a silver Toyota. Casey peered inside. The upholstery wasn't ripped, and the AC and windshield wipers worked, which was more than she could say for her Honda. Wyatt checked under the hood, then went with Casey while she test-drove the car. Fitting, as he was the one paying for it.

"It has a tilt wheel." Roy showed Casey the feature

while Wyatt looked over the outside of the car. "That'll come in handy when, you know, you expand," he muttered, gesturing to her now undisguised stomach.

"I have three months to go. I suppose I could grow a lot larger."

Wyatt heard the exchange and sent Roy a seriously irritated glance. He didn't want to be reminded of Casey's condition. That way, maybe nothing would go wrong. She said she was fine, but Wyatt knew firsthand how quickly things could change.

"I'll take it," he said. "Can we get the paperwork sorted so Casey can drive it home? Roy, if you get anything for her Honda, you and I can settle up later."

"I'll give you five hundred bucks for it," the man who'd brought the Toyota said. "Restoring cars and selling them through Roy is what I do."

"Deal," Wyatt answered, sticking out his hand.

Casey had begun to yawn before the transaction was complete. Wyatt noticed. "You look bushed. Why don't I drive? We can stop for something to eat on the way. This transaction took longer than I expected and it's way past lunchtime."

"No. You spent too much money on me already, Wyatt. We'll have to book a lot more appointments to make up for what this car cost you."

"It wasn't that expensive." He held the door while she slid into the passenger seat. "I'm comfortable with the amount of work we're doing now." He headed for the highway, and added in afterthought, "I don't want you to cram too many jobs in a day the way Angela used to. Life's about more than money, Casey."

"How do you know what's too many? I mean, every wedding is different. One may take three hours to set up and shoot, and the next may take five because of a picky mother-of-the-bride, or hungover groomsmen who straggle in too late to have their pictures taken before the ceremony."

"When you book a job don't you get a sense of those factors? For instance, you knew to allow more time at Julie Adison's wedding."

"Right. I knew her family were high muckety-mucks."

"Angela sometimes had two society weddings in a day. When we found out she was pregnant a year ago last May, I begged her not to add a single June wedding. She did anyway, because she wanted the money." Wyatt gripped the steering wheel hard. "Promise me you won't do too much."

"The holidays are right around the corner. Studios get wild, what with everyone deciding at the last minute they want family pictures for Mom, Dad and Grandma Sue."

"Why didn't that sound like a promise to take it easy?"

"Word gets out if you turn people away, Wyatt. Anyway, I hate disappointing anyone. I know my limits. I won't overdo. How's that?"

"Good. Great! There's not a lot of demand for my

kind of photography in winter. I'm available to spell you or team up if need be."

"Are you saying you'll do pictures of little kiddies with Santa's reindeer?" Casey teased.

"Very funny. I did do that one year for a church. A very moth-eaten reindeer. And don't laugh. Maybe he was a farmer's mule that someone strapped deer horns to."

Casey grinned. Wyatt seemed less tense as they drove, and she loved watching him smile. Loved the dimple that popped out in one cheek.

But then he pulled up in front of her house. He jumped out, and Casey felt the awkwardness descend again. Wyatt locked the Toyota, then dropped the keys in her hand as if it would hurt him to touch her. He climbed into his SUV and left with barely a nod good-bye.

Casey felt suddenly bereft. Darn, he was a hard man to read. When Wyatt let down his guard, Casey saw the fun-loving guy he must have been before Angela died, and was drawn to him. She was terribly afraid she could love Wyatt Keene for a lifetime. But only if her love was returned. Never again would she settle for less.

THE WEEK BEFORE THANKSGIVING was booked solid with family portraits. Most clients came to the studio. On Wednesday, Wyatt arrived shortly after noon and found Casey wrestling a phony fireplace out of the storage room. "Hey, let me get that," he said. "You shouldn't be lifting anything that heavy."

She blew an errant curl out of her eyes. "I wasn't lifting, I was scooting." She noticed Wyatt staring at her. "Do I have tinsel in my hair? I just finished using the fake Christmas tree prop for the Torres family," she explained. "By the way, Kim left you an invitation to Thanksgiving dinner. I put it on your desk. A cream-colored envelope with a gold seal. Super ritzy."

"That's Kim. Very old school." He laughed and tucked the stubborn curl behind Casey's ear. "This is the longest I've seen you wear your hair. I like it."

"Uh, thanks." Casey fluffed the back self-consciously. "I haven't had time to go for a cut. This morning, nurses at the clinic said they like it, too. I wore it pretty long when I was young. Maybe I'll be able to braid it by the time the baby comes."

Wyatt glanced at her stomach, although he'd deliberately avoiding doing so these past three weeks. If he didn't look, he could pretend she wasn't facing any threat. "You were at the clinic today? Is everything all right?"

"Routine visit. I go every other week now. I got scolded for gaining five extra pounds." She made a face. "The P.A. says, small as I am, I really need to watch my calories. He said it's too easy to overeat during the holidays."

"P.A.? Why aren't you seeing a doctor?"

"I do sometimes. That's how the clinic can afford to be free—one doctor oversees several P.As."

"Well, they're wrong. You aren't overweight in the least."

"It's all going right here. For my height, I'm a porker," she lamented. Then laughed and crossed her eyes because Wyatt looked so serious.

Expression unchanged, he slowly wrapped his arms around her. The move brought her tight against his front. "Don't make fun of being pregnant and healthy," he said fiercely. Suddenly, he broke off. "I felt your baby kick."

Embarrassed, Casey tried to pull away, but Wyatt held her fast. "I think you're going to have a star punter," he said.

"I'm still hoping for a girl," she reminded him.

"Okay. Maybe she'll be a gymnast."

"Good thing you didn't say cheerleader. That would be so Texan. All the guys who came into the brewpub bragged about their sons playing football. They were just as proud of their daughters making the cheer squad. As if those are the only two pursuits that matter."

Holding her stubborn chin lightly with his hands, Wyatt lowered his head and kissed her, drawing out the contact until they were both breathing hard.

It was a shock. Even telling herself it was wrong, Casey stood on her toes and clutched his shirt for balance. When they finally broke the kiss, Wyatt lifted his head and hauled in a deep, unsteady breath.

Casey fell back on her heels, closed her eyes and rested her forehead on his chest. She could hear the heavy thud of his heart, or maybe it was hers.

Oh, man, she wished he'd say something. But he didn't.

Finally, she cleared her throat. "Any minute now the Masons are going to walk in. They wanted to get a jump on Christmas photos, but Mrs. Mason didn't want the usual shot beside a decorated tree. That's why I went to get the fake fireplace. Why did you kiss me?" she blurted, tearing herself out of Wyatt's loose hold.

He lifted one shaky hand and rubbed the back of his neck. "Danged if I know. I broke my own rule about staying professional."

"It's okay. No harm done," Casey asserted firmly, although it cost her. "I shouldn't have griped about my weight. It was just an—"

Wyatt broke in. "If you say an aberration, I'll…kiss you again. To prove it's not. Dammit, you looked kissable, okay?"

"Okay, sheesh." She held up a hand. "Please move the fireplace into studio A." She was rattled by his comment, but couldn't count on its meaning more. If she did, she'd be disappointed when he once again kept her at arm's length. He'd been so cool and aloof lately.

Wyatt carried the faux fireplace into the front studio for her.

Taking care not to brush against him, Casey got out the garland, frosted gold tree balls and gold tapers, and arranged them on the phony mantel.

Wyatt stood back and watched, and she could sense that he wanted to say more—or explain. Thankfully, the Mason family's arrival saved them from an apology she didn't want him to make. One she didn't want to have to accept.

When she came into the back room after she'd finished the sitting, Wyatt was in his leather chair, tapping the invitation from Kim Torres against his lips. He seemed lost in thought.

Casey shoved her camera chip in the computer to upload. Wyatt turned to her. "Did Kim mention that you're included in this dinner invitation?"

Totally blindsided, she knocked over a stack of order forms. "N-no. She didn't mention it." Casey didn't want to tell him that Kim and Alec had said they'd run into him at the mall and had a conversation in which he'd apparently brought up her name several times. Alec had credited Casey with Wyatt's happier demeanor, but she'd denied it, of course.

"I can't go," she said now, bending to pick up the forms.

"Why not? Do you have other plans?"

"No, but, Wyatt, they're *your* friends first. I like Brenda and enjoy your get-togethers, but I've never tried to horn in. I've never asked any of your group to include me. I hardly know Kim and Alec." Casey got busy uploading the Mason photos.

"If I asked, would you go with me to keep me from being odd man out?"

Casey's fingers stilled. "Do you really think that's a good idea? You should know that people are already talking about us. The other day at lunch, Jana Mitchell referred to you and me as a couple, Wyatt."

"What?"

"I told Brenda I'd come clean with you about being

pregnant. Jana knew that you'd bought a car for me to drive, too. Through Roy, her blabbermouth brother-in-law."

"You didn't tell them…"

"No, of course not! I assured them that all we have is a working relationship." Biting her bottom lip, she didn't mention that Brenda and Jana had both said more than once how perfect it would be if she and Wyatt started dating.

Wyatt tossed the invitation onto his desk. "Frankly, I wish the holidays would go away. Or that I could flip the calendar to January and just get on with next year. You can't be too happy about spending Thanksgiving and Christmas alone, either. It's a hard time to be by yourself."

"Yes, but if we jumped straight to January I'd be six weeks away from having my baby. I'm not anxious to rush that. For one thing, I haven't found a labor coach. Classes at the clinic start right after Christmas and run for six weeks. I asked Brenda. She'd like to help me, but what with having three toddlers, and the holidays so close, I think she doesn't have the time. While she didn't refuse outright, she also hasn't said yes."

"Labor coach? That's where you do the panting-like-a-puppy breathing thing, right?"

"So I hear. Sounds as if you know more specifics than I do."

"I listened to the guys talk about it—they've all gone through it with their wives. Some more than once." A corner of Wyatt's mouth curved in a grin. "Dave

Mitchell fainted watching a birthing video. The guys never let him hear the end of it, until Lou Bailey told us that Wes had to run to the men's room and puke his guts out, too."

"Shame on you, laughing at the expense of your poor friends."

"Hey, I figure they're the lucky ones." Wyatt's smile disappeared. "They all got kids out of the deal," he said quietly.

"I'm sorry, Wyatt. I shouldn't have said anything. I don't know how we got there from talking about Thanksgiving dinner."

"Getting back to that, will you go with me? I'll drive to Round Rock to pick you up and take you home again. If you don't feel like it, we don't have to hang out after dinner. Generally the men head to the media room in Alec's basement to watch football. A couple of neighbor girls are hired to play with the kids. The women stay upstairs to gossip. At least that's what Angela said."

"You tempt me. I love turkey, dressing and pumpkin pie, and I didn't want to shop for all the stuff. And…I'm not supposed to overeat. This way I wouldn't have leftovers."

"So, is it a da—" Wyatt caught himself before he said the word *date* "—a deal?" he quickly amended. "If so, I'll let Alec know." Wyatt got to his feet. "The Cowboys are playing the Colts this afternoon. I may mosey on over to the Torres house and get myself invited to watch it on their big-screen TV. I ought to buy one myself. It's the next best thing to being there."

"If you give me a few minutes to crop and mat Kim and Alec's pictures, you can take them along so they won't have to make an extra trip to the studio. Grab an order form, too."

"Will you be all right here by yourself?"

Caught off guard, Casey glanced up from the photo she'd started cutting. "Why wouldn't I be?"

Wyatt rotated a shoulder negligently. "Probably because you're seven months pregnant."

"I'm fine. Pregnancy isn't an illness, Wyatt."

"You're right. I'm sorry. Are those photos almost ready to go?"

"I've got two more to mat. Look, I shouldn't have snapped. I do appreciate having you watch my back, figuratively speaking." She slid the full set of prints into a large studio envelope and passed it to him. "Other than Brenda, who's busy with her family most of the time, I don't have anyone else to count on in an emergency."

"What about your foster parents?"

"They care, of course, but Dallas is too far away to get here quickly enough. And Len's battling arthritis. Not that I expect they'll need to," she added, after noting the horrified look on Wyatt's face. "Brenda thinks I should tell Dane's parents," she admitted, feigning interest in the wall behind Wyatt. "They do have a right to know—I just feel it's Dane's place to tell them."

Wyatt jiggled the envelope as if he'd grown uncomfortable with the turn of their conversation. "I guess I'll take off for Alec's. Once you're finished with the Mason photos, go on home, why don't you? I doubt anyone will call this close to the holidays." In two strides he was at the back door. "The Torreses' invitation said cocktails at five and dinner at six. I'll pick you up tomorrow at, say, four-fifteen?"

"Sure. I assume they'll have juice or tea, not just cocktails."

"That's right. No alcohol. You must have wanted to throttle me at the Granville party when I kept insisting you have champagne."

"I wanted to tell you the truth then, and felt guilty when I couldn't work up the nerve."

"That's all behind us, Casey."

"Some people at dinner tomorrow probably still don't know. Will anyone be shocked?"

"Most will take their cues from you. Relax, Casey. Just be yourself." He offered a thin smile, then hurried out.

Casey sat back down to work, but her mind drifted. She should have asked Wyatt if the dinner would be casual or dressy. She supposed she could always call Kim. She'd been saving the green satin outfit Brenda had given her for Christmas. She'd decided to wear it even if she spent the holiday alone. Dolly had invited her to Dallas. But the Howells' sons and their families would be there. This year, Casey didn't feel like sleeping on an airbed. Now she wondered if it might be appropriate to invite Wyatt to her house for dinner. She'd already bought him a gift—an initialed leather portfolio to carry samples and order forms when he visited clients.

As she packed up to go home, she saw she still had time to stop by a maternity shop she passed almost every day. Secure in the knowledge that she had this job for as long as she needed it, she decided it would be okay to spend a little money on herself.

THE SHOP CLERKS WERE friendly, and didn't rush her even though it was the afternoon before a holiday. "You hardly show at all," the tall redhead who put Casey in a dressing room said. "The red wool dress and the rust tunic both shout that you have a bun in the oven, if that's what you want. I can also bring in a black satin pantsuit. Wear that and most people won't have a clue you're expecting." The woman dashed out and came back with the outfit.

The black satin jacket had faux diamond buttons down the front. Casey liked it, but it was outrageously expensive, and far too dressy to wear to work. "The red dress makes me feel huge," she told the clerk, and after debating, she settled on the rust tunic and a pair of black velvet pants. Yes, she looked pregnant, but not like a pregnant elephant.

"You made a good choice," the cashier said as she took Casey's money. "If you're going to wear it tomorrow, it'll keep you warm. You've probably heard we're supposed to get snow."

"Snow?" Casey clutched her purse tighter. "When we had that terrible ice storm in October, I was taking pictures at a wedding. It was so awful trying to get home! I hate to think I'd have to do that again."

The clerk shrugged. "Maybe the weatherman got it wrong. I came to work at one, though, and thought there was an added chill in the air."

Casey left, studying the sky as she hung her new purchase on a hook behind the driver's seat. Maybe she shouldn't have splurged on the outfit. If it snowed, Wyatt wouldn't be eager to drive to and from Round Rock. And for sure he'd never risk repeating what had happened during the last storm.

On and off throughout the evening, Casey listened to weather reports. Although, one forecaster mentioned possible snow for the holiday, none of the others did. She finally went to bed, wishing she'd bought food for a Thanksgiving dinner instead of a new outfit. At least it was something she could wear to photograph any of the December weddings she had scheduled. There were ten, if she recalled. Including one on Christmas Eve. When she'd booked it, she'd had doubts about how many guests would come, seeing how that was such a family time. But the bride said fifty guests had already confirmed.

If Casey ever got married again... No, she wouldn't think like that. She punched her pillow and shut off her bedside lamp.

THE NEXT DAY, SHE anxiously followed the weather. It had turned colder before she went in to shower, but the sky remained clear.

Wyatt arrived on the dot of four-fifteen. "Don't you look beautiful," he said the minute she opened the door.

"Thank you." Casey felt herself blush. Wyatt had a habit of checking her out in a way that sent heat straight through her. Nervously, she tucked a curl behind an ear, then tugged on one earlobe. She didn't often wear earrings, but today she'd put in gold hoops, and added a gold ring with a topaz stone. A gift from Dolly Howell. "Come inside," she said belatedly.

"Are you...are you ready to go?" Wyatt asked, clearing his throat.

"You bet. Oh, shoot. I forgot to buy a hostess gift."

"I have a bottle of wine in the car. It's one Kim likes a lot—we can give it together if you want."

"I'd appreciate that. Let me grab my shawl and purse, and we can go." She wasn't gone long. When she returned she saw Wyatt had turned up his jacket collar and stuffed his hands in his pockets, ready to go out in the wind.

"Where's your coat?"

"At the dry cleaners," he said. "It was a mess after the night we got soaked. I took it in and forgot until today that I hadn't picked it up. But Alec and Kim have plenty of parking near their house, so we won't have to walk far tonight."

Relieved by that news, Casey let Wyatt tuck her into the passenger seat of his SUV. She had worried that perhaps they'd be the first ones there, and it would be awkward. But Tom and Gracie Swartz, Dave and Jana Mitchell, and Emily and Ian Endress had already arrived. A few kids were running around. Some couples, like Brenda and Greg, said they had grandparents to babysit. Only Emily and Ian hadn't heard about Casey's revelation and were plainly rocked a bit at seeing her so obviously pregnant.

Emily hugged Casey. "I almost said something at the barbecue in September. I thought the outfit you had on looked like a pantsuit Brenda wore early in her pregnancy. Then I thought, *silly me.*" Lou and Wes Bailey blew in then, followed by Brenda and Greg. Any other questions Emily might have had for Casey got lost in the men's running banter. Casey soon learned Greg and Wes were the cutups of the bunch of long-time friends.

Casey had worried that she might feel out of place, but Wyatt didn't allow it. He stayed by her side the whole time.

It wasn't until after dinner, when the women pitched in to help Kim clean up and the men trooped downstairs to watch football, that Casey was on her own. Brenda sidled up to her. "What gives with you and Wyatt?"

"What do you mean? We're the same as always."

Gracie and Jana hooted, and the others stopped carting off dirty dishes to listen. Brenda raised an eyebrow suggestively. "Please. It's not a bad thing. Far from it, if you ask me. But wasn't it only a few days ago that you insisted all you and Wyatt had was a work relationship?"

"It's true."

"Like heck. Don't tell me you didn't notice how many times Wyatt slipped his arm around your waist, or put a hand on your shoulder tonight?"

Gracie nodded. "And he always noticed when your glass was empty. He went to the kitchen to get you more juice at least three times."

"He was being kind," Casey said, growing defensive. "I was nervous about coming tonight, so he was trying to make me comfortable. I mean, all of you have been friends forever. Including Angela."

"Yes, and that's why I was surprised to see Wyatt here tonight," Lou said, with a quick glance over her shoulder toward the stairs.

"It's really significant that he brought you," Emily murmured. "Last holiday season we all thought Wyatt might not survive losing Angela and the baby."

That statement sobered everyone, until Kim clapped her hands and sat them all down in the living room and began talking about Christmas plans.

Twice, Wyatt came upstairs. "Are you still doing okay?" he asked Casey the second time. "I want you to come get me if you need to leave."

"Well, no one's going anywhere before I serve the pie," Kim announced. The conversation had moved on to pregnancy and labor stories, so Casey was grateful when Kim checked her watch and hopped up from the couch. "The game probably only has a few minutes left. Em, Jana, will you help me cut pies? Gracie and Lou, check with the guys and kids to see what kind they want, will you?"

That left Brenda and Casey without chores. Casey stood, but Brenda gently pulled her back down. "I've put off telling you, Casey, but I don't see how I can manage to be your birthing coach. The Christmas chores are piling up and I'm feeling swamped. Then tonight on the way here, Greg said he'd like us to have a holiday open house for all his clients."

"It's okay, Brenda. I can phone my foster mom. Maybe she'll be able to come, after all."

"No, listen, I had a brilliant idea. Ask Wyatt to be your coach."

"Are you out of your mind? There's no way he'd agree to that!" Because the truth was, she'd mentioned needing a coach to him, and he hadn't volunteered.

"Don't dismiss it so fast. We all saw how attentive he was to you tonight. He barely took his eyes off you. There was definitely…longing. Maybe it'd be good for him to see that not all pregnancies end in disaster. Ask him, Casey."

"I can't," she sputtered as the men and older kids clomped up the stairs, ending the heart-to-heart talk.

After pie, Ian was the first to notice snowflakes falling outside the sliding glass door. Everyone crowded around, then began making excuses to leave, Casey and Wyatt among them.

Flakes fell hard and were whipped around by a brisk wind that made them feel as if they were driving in a snow globe. "It's sticking," Wyatt muttered as they reached the on-ramp to the highway. Leaning forward, he wiped the fog off the inside of the windshield, then turned up the defrosters. He pointed out a line of traffic stopped on the highway leading to Round Rock. "There must be an accident up ahead. Casey, is something wrong? You haven't said two words since we left the Torres's house."

"I was better before the women started sharing their labor stories." She didn't mention the other thing that was on her mind—Brenda's suggestion that he be her coach.

"Why would they do that and scare you?"

Casey shrugged listlessly. "Wyatt, why are you turning around?"

"Don't freak on me. I'm taking you to my house. Neither of us feels like sitting in traffic for hours. It's not as if snow here lasts for days. It'll be gone by morning. I give you my word—all I want is for us to get a good night's sleep. It won't be like last time."

Casey said nothing. She'd been shaken by the women's tales. On top of that, she was deeply disappointed that Brenda couldn't be her coach. Just now, she thought that repeating the night of the ice storm wouldn't be so bad at all.

Maybe it had been seeing the happy families this evening. The men helping their wives on with coats, and other caring signs that left Casey longing for a partner. A man with strong arms to hold her through the snowy night. Or to chase away a very real fear of having this baby by herself.

Wyatt. He would be a perfect partner, if only he could love her.

Tonight she needed someone. But Wyatt was too honorable to break his word. Casey sighed and shut her eyes.

CHAPTER ELEVEN

CASEY MADE UP HER MIND as they entered Wyatt's
house. Life was too short not to ask for what she
wanted. "Wyatt," she began, "I know you said we
wouldn't repeat history tonight. But…would you sleep
with me? Just to hold me. The guest room's fine if your
bed holds…other memories. I'm feeling, I don't
know—blue."

Her request hung between them so long, Casey
thought she'd put her foot in it. Big time put her foot
in it.

Finally, after the lengthy hesitation, Wyatt reached
out and turned her toward him. "I've totally repainted
the house and bought new furniture. There are no
memories for you to worry about," he said, taking her
shawl as he ushered her down the hall to his bedroom.

Once there, Casey felt funny. Wyatt's bed, his room,
loomed in front of her. She wished she could snatch
back her bold words. What had she been thinking?
Wyatt had probably given in because she'd sounded
so…needy. She paused at the threshold. "Maybe this
wasn't such a good idea."

"It was a very good idea," Wyatt said, his voice rough with emotion.

She clutched the front of her new tunic. "If you'll lend me your shirt again, I can change in the bathroom." She pointed down the hall toward the guest bathroom she'd used last time.

"Casey, I know what it's like to be lonely and sad." He held her gaze as he shed his jacket and began unbuttoning his shirt. "We'll just sleep," he said.

Grateful for the comfort he offered, she moved toward him. "I accept."

His bed was wide and comfortable, and his body radiated heat. Sleeping in Wyatt's arms gave Casey the best night she could remember. She could easily make a habit of sleeping with Wyatt—if only he loved her.

DAYS LATER, IT SEEMED that the incredible, snowy night had created a noticeable shift in Wyatt's attentiveness. Casey couldn't put her finger on it, but he began accompanying her to wedding shoots without her asking. Although he still changed the subject whenever she mentioned anything to do with the baby, which was disheartening.

The second week in December, she arrived at the studio later than usual. "I forgot to tell you I had a nine o'clock appointment at the clinic this morning," she said, before Wyatt could ask where she'd been.

"Is there a problem? You had a clinic appointment last Tuesday."

"I'm going every week from now until the baby comes."

"Oh," he said when Casey went straight to work on a photograph.

"Everything's normal," she told him when Wyatt said nothing more. "The nurse is pleased with my weight. She says I've done well, but I'll need to be careful with Christmas around the corner. Speaking of Christmas, I finally put up a tree. I imagine, late as it is, you've already made plans to spend the holiday with friends."

"No, no plans yet. Uh, I thought about inviting you to dinner." Wyatt twisted his lips wryly. "I can't cook anything fancy. But we could go out," he said quickly. "We could probably still get a reservation somewhere."

"Mercy, I can cook. My place or yours?"

Wyatt frowned. "I can't ask you to spend all day in the kitchen, especially since we've got that Christmas Eve wedding the night before."

"You didn't ask—I volunteered. I've thought about inviting you over for Christmas dinner ever since Thanksgiving, but we've been so busy. Or we can go out," she added, because it was easy to see he was really against her having to cook. A sudden thought struck her and she snapped her fingers. "I know! What if I come to your house at, say, ten? I'll make a stollen for breakfast. We can have that before we exchange gifts. Oh, crap! That came out wrong. I bought you a token present, Wyatt. I'm not hinting for you to buy me one."

He came over to where she sat at the computer, laid

a finger over her mouth, then lifted her out of the chair and kissed her. When after several minutes he sat her back down, she knew her eyes were sparkling. "I already have your gift," he said gruffly. "But what the hell is a stollen?"

Her lips felt delightfully numb, but she managed to say, "It's a German sweet bread. I used to make it for Dane's family each year. The bread is glazed and inside there are raisins, nuts and bits of citrus. I wish I hadn't mentioned Dane's folks. They sent me a gift but all I sent them was a card."

"They know you're divorced, don't they?"

"Yes, but until this gift came, I'd had only one letter from Dane's mother, scolding me for not being a more understanding wife to her son."

"I take it if whatsizname is still off climbing mountains, then he hasn't told them that he's about to become a father."

"He's *not* going to be a father," Casey said, irritated.

Wyatt shifted his gaze to the ceiling, as he often did when conversation turned to Casey's ex or the baby. It frustrated her even more when his next sentence was some stupid comment about the weather.

"Can you believe these warm temperatures, after ice in October and snow in November?"

"That's right," she snapped, banging on the computer keys. "Let's talk about the weather, but never about the fact I'm going to be a single mother in less than two months."

Wyatt arched an eyebrow. "I was about to ask you

how patio dining on Christmas Day sounds. I know just the place. Bring your stollen for the morning and I'll make dinner reservations."

Casey knew she was acting bitchy. It probably came with feeling fat and hormonal. She opened her mouth to suggest they forget dinner, since she wouldn't be good company, but their first appointment of the day came in, ending their exchange.

That was the last chance they had to talk. Everyone who'd booked December appointments wanted their photos before Christmas. Casey and Wyatt put in extra hours every day, often passing in the parking lot as each went a different direction.

Two days before Christmas, Wyatt was heading out to deliver packets to three customers when he paused at the computer where Casey worked feverishly on a composite for a newly engaged couple. "It doesn't make much sense for you to drive all the way home after the Caldwell wedding, just to drive back the next morning. Feel free to pack a bag and spend the night at my house. Or two nights. Christmas Eve and Christmas."

He was out the back door and gone before Casey collected her senses. Was that an invitation to sleep with him again? Her chest constricted and her breathing became shallow. Curling up in Wyatt's arms could cure her discontent. She shouldn't, a little voice nagged. Since their last tense discussion, Casey had decided it was understandable for Wyatt to be a bit annoyed if

Dane's name came up. But it wasn't okay for him to avoid the subject of her baby.

If he had issues, she wished he'd spell them out. The further along she got in her pregnancy, the more she sensed Wyatt wanted to ignore the fact that she'd soon be a mother. For that reason, and since the weather was supposed to be clear, Casey decided she'd drive home after the wedding.

The next day he acted surprised when she told him she intended to spend the night at home. "Okay, but it seems a waste of gas to me."

Several times during the Caldwell reception, Casey noticed Wyatt watching her with a brooding expression.

He insisted on walking her to her car. "I want you to call me when you get in, Casey. I don't care how late it is. I won't sleep easy until I know you made it home safe."

"I'm a good driver," she said, slamming the rear door after tossing in her camera.

"No argument there." He scraped her curls out from under her collar. "I'm worried about the others. A lot of people will be drinking tonight." His hands lingered on her shoulders. He bent and dropped a kiss on her nose. When she leaned into him, Wyatt moved his lips to hers until they got a whistle from some young guys leaving the reception. He stepped back and opened her door. "Call me. And think about bringing an overnight bag tomorrow."

Driving home alone, Casey regretted her decision not to stay with him tonight.

EARLY THE NEXT MORNING she was glad for her resolve. The Howells phoned to wish her a happy holiday. "I'm making the stollen recipe you gave me to take a friend's home, Dolly. The dough is almost ready, so I can't talk long. I feel fine, Dolly. Thank you for the scarf and the receiving blankets," she said.

After she hung up, she toyed with the idea of calling them back to tell them about Wyatt. But she didn't, because Dolly would have questions that Casey couldn't answer.

PULLING INTO WYATT'S driveway a few hours later, Casey set aside her feelings of guilt. She was determined to enjoy the day and breezed into his house without any constraints. She'd phoned ahead and asked him to preheat the oven. The first thing she did was put the bread in and set the timer.

"That stuff you're baking sure smells good," Wyatt said once they were settled at his kitchen table with hot drinks. "Did I mention how pretty you look in that green dress?"

"Three times." She smiled at him over the rim of her teacup.

"I have something for you," he said. "It'll go nicely with what you're wearing. I, ah, hope you like it." He pulled a small wrapped package out of his pocket. Casey's heart fluttered. She set her cup on the table to keep from dropping it.

"I put your gi-gift under the tree," she stammered. "As I said, it's nothing big."

Wyatt pressed the package into her trembling hands. he unwrapped it with difficulty, and popped open the id on a white leather jewelry box. Inside, nestled on vhite velvet, lay a gold necklace with a pendant of a nother holding an infant—a curly haired girl. It wasn't vhat Casey expected. It was far more. Her eyes blurred vith tears. Her hands shook as she tried to fasten the elicate chain around her neck, so Wyatt did it for her, hen kissed her neck.

"Do you like it?" he asked, his voice a low rumble ear her ear.

"It's beautiful." She cradled the pendant in her right and. "I'll wear it every day for luck. Luck with my elivery," she murmured.

"I know you want a girl. I haven't asked, but I take : you don't know what you're having. Couldn't they ll from the ultrasounds?"

"They probably could, but I didn't really want to now. Anyway, it doesn't matter." She gripped the pen- ant tighter. "Would it matter to you, Wyatt?"

"It's nothing to do with me." He scowled, his gaze rifting to her belly.

"I desperately need a birthing coach," Casey blurted. I don't want to go alone, but I can't afford to miss a ngle class."

"I know. Brenda's been nagging me to volunteer," Vyatt said. "I didn't think you'd want a strange guy ıere."

"I want *you*. You're not a stranger. Please, Wyatt. I now it's a lot to ask."

Out of the blue, he rested a hand on her stomach. "I—I...let's get married," he stammered.

Casey's world tilted. "Why?" she asked, trying to keep him in focus. More than anything she wanted Wyatt to say he loved her. She willed him to say the words, even though she was afraid he might see the longing in her tear-filled eyes.

"I, uh, told you before. I want kids. I've always wanted a big family. I have this house and..."

Crushed, Casey stepped away from him and bumped into the stove. Her joy drained out of her. She really, truly, wished she could accept. Wished they could be a family. But no words of love had crossed Wyatt's lips.

Obviously she hadn't been what Dane wanted in a wife. But she'd be darned if she'd walk into another one-sided marriage. "I wasn't begging for a husband, Wyatt, only a labor coach."

She could barely handle looking at him, and was hugely relieved when the stove buzzer went off announcing the stollen was done. She quickly grabbed the oven mitts, and hid her face as she bent to pull the bread from the oven.

PUZZLED BY CASEY'S ANGRY movements, Wyatt went to the cupboard for the plates. It was painfully obvious that more than the stollen had cooled. In spite of the heat from the oven, there was a decided chill in his kitchen.

They managed to get through the rest of the day, though it wasn't easy. Wyatt thanked Casey several times for the leather carrying case. She did the same after he treated her to an expensive dinner, during which they hardly spoke. The hotel dining room was decked out with groupings of white trees that glittered icily with silver bells only adding to the atmosphere. Thankfully, the drive back to Wyatt's house was short. He hadn't hung a single decoration, which told Casey a lot when she stopped to think about it.

"I'll be your coach if you still need one," he said abruptly as they stood beside her car. There was no chance she'd agree to stay over now.

She straightened after putting her overnight bag in the backseat. "Don't go out of your way. I can ask Dolly Howell to come down from Dallas."

"Six weeks is a long visit and you said her husband isn't in great health. I want to do it, Casey," Wyatt insisted.

"Fine, but if you faint or throw up, don't blame me." With that she left.

THEY KEPT BUSY AT WORK for the next few days, again staying out of each other's way. So much so that Casey had to leave a sticky note on Wyatt's desk giving him the date and time of the first class. He never responded, so when she went to the specified room in the basement of the hospital, she wasn't at all sure he'd show up. But in fact he beat her there. They sat next to each other, careful to keep their shoulders from touching.

A freckle-faced nurse named Tori Evans breezed in, greeting each woman individually. She had folders with the forms each mother had filled out. Casey had added Wyatt's name as her coach on Monday. When Tori asked if he was the baby's father, Casey regretted having to say that he wasn't.

"Coaches, relax," Tori said with a grin. "The goal of birthing classes is to increase each woman's confidence in her ability to give birth. By the end of these six weeks, the moms will learn how to respond to pain in ways that facilitate labor and increase their comfort." She stepped to a TV set at one end of the room. "I know you're all nervous about the birth process, so we'll get through the hardest part first. Tonight we'll watch a video of real deliveries, and our next sessions will be worry free."

Casey turned toward Wyatt. "You don't have to do this."

He said nothing, but settled more firmly into his uncomfortable metal chair.

Halfway through the video, Wyatt glanced at Casey and noticed her face had gone pale. Without a word, he reached for her clenched fists and eased them apart. "Who's the nervous one now?" he whispered in her ear.

She tried to pull away, but he linked his fingers with hers. When the video was over, Tori chatted with the coaches as each couple left the room. "Welcome," she said to Wyatt. "You did well tonight. Better than some who ducked out. Casey, you seemed very tense. Don't worry. You'll find it easier to relax after Wyatt learns the massage techniques."

Casey sputtered, then lowered her head and dashed

down the hall. Wyatt ran to catch up. "What was all that about?"

"Massage? I can't believe Tori said that. She knows you're not my husband."

"No, I'm not," he said shortly. "But you still need a coach. Do you want me to stay or not?"

Casey let three other couples go past before she kicked at a loose floor tile and said, "Yes. Yes, thank you."

Wyatt wisely left it at that. Their next class wasn't until after the new year, so they had a few days' hiatus.

ON NEW YEAR'S EVE, Wyatt and Casey both attended the party at Lou and Wes Bailey's house, but drove separately. Somehow word had spread that Wyatt was partnering Casey at her classes. Greg Moore pulled him aside early in the evening and handed him a beer. "A toast to a new year. To getting on with your life. Brenda's been asking, since you're doing childbirth classes with Casey, does that mean there's something more going on with you two—maybe something more romantic? I guess we're wondering."

"I asked her to marry me. Christmas Day." Wyatt stared glumly at his drink. "I thought I was reading her right, but she turned me down flat. She acted upset."

"Being pregnant can make a woman totally irrational over the strangest things."

"I thought she'd want to be married before the baby comes. I want her and the baby to be my family," Wyatt stressed. "I told her I wanted us all to be together. At least I think I did," he mumbled, setting his untouched beer on the counter. "Truth is, Greg, I'm afraid to put my heart on the line again."

"You've got it bad, Wyatt. If you love her, you'll have to try harder to convince her."

Greg's mention of love rattled Wyatt. He'd loved Angela and their speck of an unborn baby. His heart had been broken when he'd lost them. Then Casey came along, and his pain eased and eventually went away. He cared a lot for her—for her welfare. Right then it hit him—the weight in his chest was love. He would love her and want to be her husband even if there was no baby. Boy, he'd bungled it the other day, and now he had to figure out how to tell her. She'd gotten good at not being alone with him. He'd just find a way to do it right.

WYATT BOUGHT A RING the second week of January. He carried it around with him as he spent his days at work showing Casey how much he cared about her. He ran all the errands, and carried the props she needed to the sitting room before she requested them. He even checked out the locations of the off-site jobs, and didn't schedule Casey for anywhere she'd have to lug her equipment up stairs.

One blustery day toward the end of January, Casey packed her camera bag for a wedding she'd planned to shoot alone, only to discover Wyatt getting ready to join her. She spun on him, and shouted, "Stop it! Stop it, Wyatt. You're smothering me. I'm not a hothouse flower. I'm a grown woman and I can take care of myself."

Hurt, Wyatt lashed out. "You're a woman who's almost nine months pregnant. This wedding is all the way in Spring Prairie—halfway to Houston. Going there alone is too risky. Where's your cell phone? On the charger, right? You've got to be more careful. Dammit, you know how badly things can go wrong."

"The doctor and P.A. say I'm fine. Don't mix me up with Angela, Wyatt." Casey stormed off, but her words hit him like a slap. He hadn't thought about Angela since New Year's Day. Only Casey. Who massaged her back and legs in class? Who listened to the nurse talk about possible complications? He did, and Casey should have been paying attention, too.

ON THE FIRST DAY OF February, Wyatt stood at the counter in the studio, cropping photos he'd taken at a dog show. Once again, like as many times lately, he was trying to work up the nerve to get down on one knee and offer Casey his love, his name and the ring—and cut through the icy barriers she'd erected since Christmas.

She sat at the computer in back printing pictures she'd taken the day before of a brand-new baby and mom. The subjects made her weepy, but Wyatt was afraid to offer comfort in case she bit his head off. Maybe this wasn't the best time, he thought, patting his pocket to make sure he still had the ring.

The front door suddenly opened. An older couple

and a man about Wyatt's age walked in, letting a brisk wind blow through the studio. Wyatt threw an arm across his photos.

At the sound of the bell and Wyatt's curse, Casey came out from the back.

Wyatt sensed her behind him, heard her quick intake of breath and turned to look. "Casey?" He slipped an arm around her waist, thinking she'd gone white enough to faint.

Her eyes were glued to the group at the counter. "D-Dane. Mr. and Mrs. Sinclair," she said in a strained voice. "W-what are you doing here?"

Wyatt continued to hold her up, but shock rendered him speechless. He wanted to toss the lot of them out on their fancy backsides. They had some nerve showing up when Casey was an emotional wreck at this stage in her pregnancy.

Suzette Sinclair, a tall, elegantly groomed woman, set her designer handbag right on top of Wyatt's photos while she removed her leather gloves. "Casey, dear. Dane only arrived home from his travels yesterday. Imagine Richard's and my shock to learn you two are expecting a baby. We know our son can be impetuous. But I'm very surprised by you, Casey. Why on earth didn't *you* tell us?"

Casey sagged against Wyatt, who tightened his hand on her waist and hugged her to him more closely.

"And who is this?" Suzette asked, running a dismissive eye over Wyatt.

"Uh, this is Wyatt Keene. He owns the studio. Wyatt,

meet my ex-husband and his parents. Dane, Suzette and Richard Sinclair." Casey struggled to be polite. She clung to Wyatt, grabbing his arm tightly when he tried to release her after the introductions.

Richard Sinclair clamped a beefy hand around the back of his son's neck and pushed him forward. Dane continued to stare angrily at the floor. Richard's lips thinned. "Casey, you're exactly what this young idiot needs. A wife and child will ground him. He's assured me he has the wanderlust out of his system. Tell her, Dane."

But the minute Dane looked up at her, Casey knew not one thing about him had changed. She'd never seen a man less eager to be saddled with a wife and baby. Not that she would ever take him back.

Suzette stepped forward and laid a hand on her son's shoulder. "Yes, tell her, Dane. Tell Casey about the deal you and your father worked out. She comes back to Dallas, you remarry, and we'll see you have a nice place to live. And Casey," she chirped, "Dane's agreed to work in the family business. There's no need to rely on that silly pub anymore. We understand you two may need to patch up some hard feelings, but Richard and I will do everything we can to help you salvage your marriage. After all, you'll soon be giving birth to our first grandchild."

Wyatt let go of Casey so quickly, it was as if it hurt him to touch her. He shoved Mrs. Sinclair's expensive handbag aside and hastily scraped together his photographs. Dumping them under the counter, he grabbed his camera and left the studio without a word.

Casey recognized the flash of raw pain in Wyatt's eyes. But she had to deal with the immediate problem first. She was furious with Dane. His surly attitude, and the fact that he didn't so much as say hello, shouted that there was no chance he wanted to mend his ways.

"Mr. and Mrs. Sinclair, I'm so sorry we hurt you by keeping this from you. I felt Dane should be the one to tell you. I'm also sorry you've wasted your time driving down here. It's over between Dane and me. There is no marriage to salvage."

Dane shot her a dirty look, but he snatched up his mother's purse and gloves. "I told you both that, but you wouldn't listen. Can't you see she doesn't want to marry me again, any more than I want to marry her? You saw that guy, her boss. I'll bet he's not *just* her boss," he added with a sneer.

"Shut up, Dane." Casey pounded a fist on the counter. "Don't you dare criticize Wyatt. It's thanks to him I have food on my table and a roof over my head. Did you tell your parents how you left me—and your unborn baby—with no money and no income?" She held fast to the counter as Dane quickly herded his parents out of the studio before she could say more.

Casey was already sobbing in fury and frustration when a pain tore through her abdomen. Crying out, she sagged against the counter. She needed to calm down. She'd been experiencing Braxton Hicks contractions on and off for the past week. She hadn't told Wyatt, but she'd mentioned them to Tori Evans at their last class. Tori explained that the contractions were from the baby moving into position for delivery. So Casey was fairly confident that this new intensity had simply been caused by the confrontation with the Sinclairs.

Nevertheless, Tori had said that if there was any change, Casey should go to the clinic to be checked out. She scribbled a note to Wyatt, in case he came back to the studio. If she didn't hear from him by the time she finished at the clinic, she'd track him down. She needed to set him straight about what had just happened.

Propping up the note where Wyatt was sure to see it, she reached for her jacket. A second pain struck, even more intense than the last. It nearly drove Casey to her knees. She felt a ripple of fear. If these were actual labor pains, they were two weeks early.

She needed Wyatt. No matter how many times she'd accused him of being over protective, she was scared, and he was the only person whose help she wanted.

She'd already reached for her phone when her water broke. Her baby was going to make his or her entrance early. Casey fought pain and fear, yet all she could think was how badly she needed Wyatt. As another pain tore through her, she pressed the speed dial button with shaking hands and prayed he'd take her call.

WYATT HAD DRIVEN FOUR or so blocks from the studio when he asked himself what he thought he was doing. He was acting like a jerk—no better than Dane. Casey hadn't wanted him to go. She'd clutched his arm, and he'd seen the pleading look in her eyes. He knew he was going back. His love for Casey and her baby was strong enough to stand up to the Sinclairs.

After making an illegal U-turn, Wyatt was on his way to the studio when his cell rang. He glanced at the call display and his heart leaped as he saw Casey's name.

The strain in her voice as she told him she was in labor made him press harder on the accelerator. "Hang on, babe. It's okay. It's okay. Breathe deep. Casey, honey, I was already on my way back."

Wyatt roared into the parking lot, and left his car door standing open. He burst into the studio, ready to do battle with the whole Sinclair clan. He found Casey alone, curled up on the floor, chanting his name.

"Here, let me help you up. Calm down. Did you call an ambulance? What do you need?"

"I need you, Wyatt. I…my water broke a few minutes…several minutes ago. The pains are really close together now. Will you phone the hospital and let them know to expect me? I'm sorry…so sorry to put you through this." She broke off and started the breathing they'd practiced.

Wyatt cradled her in his arms. Using the techniques he'd learned in the classes, he calmed himself and Casey, then called for an ambulance.

Wyatt soothed her with encouraging words, and held her hand as the ambulance arrived minutes later and sped them both to the hospital.

He tried not to panic as nurses whisked Casey away and ordered him to wait until they had her settled. He shoved his hands in his pockets and felt the ring he'd bought. He pulled it out, but dropped it and it bounced across the floor. He retrieved it and when the nurse beckoned, he tucked it in his shirt pocket and hurriedly followed her down the hall. He took a seat in the chair next to Casey's bed. "It's okay, sweetheart," he murmured, wiping the sweat from her pale face. "We're going to get through this together. And everything's going to be okay."

"I trust you, Wyatt. There's no person in the world I trust more."

That was the last of their private conversation as things moved quickly. The doctor on call, not the doctor Casey knew, came in, checked her and announced she was crowning. Within minutes, the OB passed Wyatt a pair of scissors to cut the cord of the red, squalling infant.

"You have your girl," Wyatt whispered, kissing Casey's forehead as the nurse set the baby on her chest.

"Is she okay?" Casey asked shakily.

"She's small, but she has great lungs," the doctor said with a grin. "We'll get a weight and measure. If her appetite is as healthy as her lungs, you two can take her home in a couple of days, and enjoy being parents."

"Oh, but I'm—" Wyatt started to say he wasn't the baby's father, but Casey gripped his hand so hard, he broke off midsentence.

"You are the only father my baby has, Wyatt. You stood by me when I needed you. You helped usher her into the world."

He hesitated, watching two nurses bustle about, cleaning the baby, weighing her and bundling her to tuck into the crook of Casey's arm.

Listening to Casey coo lovingly at her daughter, Wyatt couldn't hold back his concerns another moment. "What about the Sinclairs? Do you want me to notify them?"

"I assume they went back to Dallas. I don't know for sure. Tomorrow, if you have time, you can hunt up their home number, and inform Suzette and Richard they have a granddaughter. I should tell Dane myself, though I made it very clear he and I are finished. I'm willing to bet everything I own that he'll never make an effort to see me or his child again. I'm sorry for him that he won't know his daughter, but I have to believe we're all better off this way."

"And how are you? I can't even tell you how scared I was when you called, and then to find you on the floor like that…"

"It's over, Wyatt. It was nowhere near as bad as I'd feared."

"I'm glad. Really glad." Relieved, Wyatt squeezed her free hand and said, "If you have a cell number for the Sinclairs, I'll call them now."

"Hang on. I'll see if I can remember Suzette's number." She thought a moment and rattled it off.